CW00520491

Skobeloff Horror & Ghost Stories Anthology

Horror & Ghost Stories Anthology

First edition
Compiled and edited by
Joram van Hartingsveldt

October 2023

Copyright
Skobeloff Horror & Ghost Stories Anthology

© Skobeloff Publishing 2023
© Barlow Crassmont 2023
© C.S. Dines 2023
© Callum Melvein 2023
© David Maguire 2023
© Elizabeth Butler 2023
© Elizabeth Catherine 2023
© Frederick Pangbourne / Pangbourne Estate 2023
© Ivan Richardson 2023
© James Hancock 2023
© Jarick Weldon 2023
© Jim Gilbert 2023
© Jonah Jones 2023
© Kathy Goddard 2023
© Kenneth Walker 2023
© Mark Konik 2023
© Masimba Musodza 2023
© Matthew Tett 2023
© Michael Noonan 2023
© Phill Campbell 2023
© Poppy Whitworth 2023
© Robin Kilmister 2023
© S.L. Markham 2023
© Sue Gerrard 2023
© Susan Temple 2023
© WR James 2023

The moral rights of the authors have been asserted.

ISBN 979-8-85-801762-2
Imprint: Independently published
First published worldwide in October 2023

Skobeloff Publishing
https://skobeloff.uk/

All rights reserved. No part of this publication may be reproduced, stored in a retrieval system, or transmitted, in any form or by any means, without the prior permission of Skobeloff Publishing and the individual authors or their estate, or as expressly permitted by law, by licence or under terms agreed with the appropriate reprographics rights organisation.

This is a work of fiction. Names, characters, places, and incidents either are the product of the authors' imaginations or are used fictitiously. Any resemblence to actual persons—living or dead, events, or locales is entirely coincidental.

All stories in this book are printed with permission from the copyright holders.

Preface

Joram van Hartingsveldt

In the dimly lit corners of our existence, where the shadows dance and the unknown whispers, lies an enduring fascination—a fascination that has lurked within us since time immemorial. Humans have always been drawn to the eerie and the inexplicable, seeking solace and thrill in tales that send shivers cascading down the spine.

As we approach the eerie eve of Halloween, when the boundary between the living and the departed is said to waver, or as we gather round firesides at Christmas, sharing stories of restless spirits, we are reminded of our innate yearning for the supernatural. These are the moments when the veil separating the world of the living from the realm of the beyond thins, and we become keenly aware of the spectral possibilities lurking just beyond our understanding.

But not all ghost stories are meant to terrify. Some reveal the tender strands that connect us to the afterlife—a longing to communicate, to understand what lies beyond the curtain of existence, and to grapple with the enigma of life's mysteries. These tales, whether spine-chilling or heartwarming, illuminate the peculiar bond between the living and the dearly departed.

In this anthology, one will find a medley of the strange and the unusual, a tribute to our insatiable curiosity about the dark and shadowy corners of existence. If you dare to peer into the abyss, to confront the unknown and the unseen, and to journey into the realm not meant for mortals to enter, turn these pages with caution. For within them, you will encounter stories that will haunt your dreams and leave you pondering the mysteries of life, death, and the ever-present spectre of the afterlife.

Acknowledgements

The publisher wishes to extend their gratitude to the following people and organisations, without whom this anthology would not have been possible.

- Almond Press
  - https://dystopianstories.com/
- Seen and Done, Peter Hankins
  - https://seen-and-done.com/
- Artinfoland
  - https://artinfoland.com/
- artist-led in St Helens
  - https://www.instagram.com/artistledsthelens/
- Claire Weetman
  - https://www.instagram.com/claireweetman/
- Kaouther Bouali
- Robert Pangborn
- Sophie Williamson at St Helens CDP
- All artists who submitted their work
- Gordon Johnson (GDJ)
  - https://pixabay.com/users/gdj-1086657/
  - https://pixabay.com/vectors/divider-flourish-line-art-separator-7551961/
  - https://pixabay.com/vectors/divider-separator-flourish-line-art-5845199/
  - https://pixabay.com/vectors/vintage-frame-line-art-antique-old-4509873/
  - https://pixabay.com/vectors/skull-crossbones-line-art-death-7443688/
- Igino Marini
  - https://www.1001fonts.com/im-fell-english-font.html
- Bumbayo Font Fabrik
  - https://www.1001fonts.com/gruen-lemonograf-font.html

Contents

About the Authors...xi

The Attic Room..1   C.S. Dines
Silver Roses..13   Poppy Whitworth
The Head Gardner..19   Masimba Musodza
The Reflection In My Soul.....................................29   Elizabeth Butler
Christmas Dinner..35   Sue Gerrard
Twelve Shells...41   James Hancock
The Ghost of Home...49   Elizabeth Catherine
Hog Fever...53   Phill Campbell
The Cormorant...59   Mark Konik
Movement Detected...65   Frederick Pangbourne
Out of Ancient Wallachia......................................71   Jonah Jones
Doggone...91   S.L. Markham
Deathtrap...97   Jarick Weldon
Scrooge's Chain..105   Kathy Goddard
The Black Sheep..117   Michael Noonan
Ward 5C..133   Susan Temple
Him..141   Jim Gilbert
Just Before the War in Ukraine...............................155   WR James
Never Put Yourself Into Your Art!............................173   Robin Kilmister
Pretty Pieces..181   David Maguire
One Big Treat..189   Matthew Tett
An Ill-Fated Journey...193   Kenneth Walker
Lurking Behind...205   Ivan Richardson
An Unoccupied House..211   Barlow Crassmont
An Oldie, But Not a Goodie...................................219   Callum Melvein

About the Authors

C.S. Dines

C.S. Dines is in his early fifties, of mixed heritage, and lives/works in Essex, UK. His published and forthcoming flash fiction, short stories and poetry can be found via PsychoToxin Press, The Mocking Owl Roost, D&T Publishing, Red Polka Books, CAAB Publishing, Wicked Shadow Press, Rock and Roll Nightmares, Altered Reality, David Cairns Publishing, Culture-Cult, Forward Press and Eye to the Telescope. Additionally, he loves hats, ragtime and plays the banjolele rather badly ...

Poppy Whitworth

Poppy Whitworth is an aspiring writer with a particular interest in the horror genre. Having gained her degree in Theatre Design at university in 2012, she has gone on to do multiple creative projects, including illustrating. Her love for people and everyday life has led her to a career in care, where she is inspired by the people and places around her. Poppy has a short flash fiction piece published in another anthology, *Flashes of Nightmare*.

Masimba Musodza

Masimba Musodza is a published author of some note. He was born in Zimbabwe, but has lived much of his adult life in the UK, particularly Middlesbrough, North East England. Masimba's short fiction, mostly on the speculative fiction spectrum, has appeared in anthologies and periodicals around the world, such as *Omenana, Winter Tales, AfroSFv3*, etc. He has two novels and a novella in ChiShona, his first language, and a collection of stories in English.

- https://masimbamusodza.uk/ (available late October 2023)
- Facebook: https://www.facebook.com/MasimbaMusodzaAuthor
- ISFDB: https://www.isfdb.org/cgi-bin/ea.cgi?230825

Elizabeth Butler

Elizabeth Butler is a disabled writer using a wheelchair. She has a Masters Degree in Creative Writing, has been featured in a poetry anthology, and has a collection of children's stories published online. She has self-published several books of poetry and achieved recognition in her local area and has performed at local events.

- Instagram: @eabwriting_
- TikTok: @eabwriter

Sue Gerrard

Sue Gerrard has had published twenty-three books including eleven poetry collections, two ghost novellas and a collection of ghost stories. She has also had published nine Local History books, some of which are published by Amberley Publishing. She was recently runner up in the NAWG Open Poetry and Ghost Story competitions. She has read at the Edinburgh Fringe Festival, the Royal Exchange Theatre, Manchester and many other festivals. In 2023 she has read at Clitheroe Castle among other places. In February she was awarded 'Pride of Merseyside' by Radio Merseyside for her services to writing and poetry.

She was awarded and took up the 'Robert Lord Writing Residency' in Dunedin, New Zealand in 2018/19. Pear Tress Press, New Zealand published *Poems for the Cottage* based on her stay there. Copies of these are held in major New Zealand libraries.

- https://suegerrard.com/

James Hancock

James Hancock is a writer/screenwriter who specialises in bizarre comedy, thriller, horror, sci-fi and twisted fairy tales. He takes readers down strange and seldom trodden paths, often dark, and always with a twist or two along the way. A few of his short screenplays have been made into films, his stories read on podcasts, and he has been published in several print magazines, online, and in anthology books.

He lives in England with his wife, two daughters, and a bunch of pets he insisted his girls could NOT have.

• X (formerly Twitter): @JimHank13

Elizabeth Catherine

Elizabeth Catherine is currently working on her writing in her spare time, while looking for work.

Phill Campbell

Phill Campbell has been writing since he could hold a pen and scribble on a blank page. Phill specialises in short stories in the genres of sci-fi, supernatural horror and Southern Gothic. His work has won competitions like the Writer's News, and has been featured in publications like *Pipeline Magazine* and *Woman's Own*.

Mark Konik

Mark Konik is a writer from Newcastle, Australia. His plays and short stories have been published and performed in Australia, The UK, The US, UAE, Canada, India and New Zealand. The short film he wrote, *A Million Times Before*, was produced in San Francisco and was selected for several film festivals in Europe and North America.

Frederick Pangbourne

Frederick Pangbourne was a short horror story author with five anthologies in publication. He has stories featured in various magazines, anthologies and audio podcasts. Frederick passed away in 2023, shortly before the release of this anthology. His brother wrote the following in memoriam for this book.

Frederick Pangbourne (1967-2023)

My brother and I were weaned on Drive-In B flicks and *Chiller Theatre* late night horror movies. Our father was a voracious reader of horror and golden age sci-fi, who instilled in both of us a great love for the likes of Stephen King, HP Lovecraft, Richard Matheson, Fritz Leiber, Robert Bloch ... You are likely to get a glimpse of many of these early influences peppered throughout Fred's work. Dad, were he alive today, would be as I am, beside himself with pride and bursting with happiness to see that in the later years of his life, my brother fully embraced his gift.

After proudly serving in the Marine Corps and twenty years of working in federal law enforcement, Fred was finally able to retire and do what he loved. In a very short but creatively explosive period of time before his all too soon passing, my brother was able to get his stories featured in countless magazines, anthologies, audio books and podcasts.

He will be sorely missed by all of us that loved him, but there is a great deal of consolation in knowing he will now live on through these stories.

You did it Bro. Now rest in peace.

RF Pangborn

Jonah Jones

Jonah Jones lives in South Wales, UK.

As a writer—film: One short script produced. Co-writer on two more. One script in production, one in post-production. Both feature-length and short scripts have won awards. Published: Short stories, articles and abstracts. Stage: Eight plays produced. Radio: Three Short stories and two plays broadcast (BBC). Various pieces for Radio 2, Radio 4 and Radio Wales. Series and programme for Radio Wales. TV: Sketches and short scripts for S4C, BBC. On-line monologue.

As a director—three short films and a documentary. All short films have won awards. Another short film in post-production.

S.L. Markham

S.L. Markham is an aspiring author from the United Kingdom who spends more time thinking about writing than actually doing it. She hopes this isn't the only time you see her name published in a book.

Jarick Weldon

Jarick Weldon is the pseudonym of a writer based in Yorkshire and Galloway. In his other life, he is a medical doctor and scientist. He started storywriting 'seriously' in late 2022. Since then, has had several short stories published and a shortlisting in the annual *HG Wells Short Story Competition*. He is currently studying for an MA in creative writing. Jarick's particular interests are science fiction, the paranormal, historical myths, and humorous encounters. He has a wife, cats, and an interest in Buddhism.

Kathy Goddard

Kathy lives in South Lincolnshire and is a member of the Red Wine Writers group. They introduced her to her mentor, Sue Burge, who is helping her to shape her psychological suspense novel ready to start the submission process. Alongside the novel, she continues to enter short story competitions. She has had successes with the Writing Magazine and

Writers' Forum, and also had a short horror story published with Enchanted Forest. She enters Fictionette's monthly competitions, and has had some of her stories published on their website.

- Facebook: https://www.facebook.com/kathryn.goddard.50767/
- Instagram: @goddard9467
- X (formerly Twitter): @KathyGoddard9

Michael Noonan

Michael Noonan lives in Halifax (home of the Piece Hall), West Yorkshire, has a background in food production, retail and office work.

He has had stories published in the anthology volumes *Even More Tonto Stories* and *Shades of Sentience*. A fairy-tale he penned, entitled *The Guardian of the Wood*, has been published in the *Fantasy Arts and Studies Journal* in France, and a story he wrote, called *The Personality Cult*, has been published by *Terror House Magazine*, based in Budapest, Hungary.

His short story *The Labyrinth* was printed in the anthology volume *Colp: Underground* in Australia, and his tale *All the Time in the World* has been published in *Fission #2 Volume 1: Stories from the British Science Fiction Association*.

Michael has had a book of stories published, titled *Seven Tall Tales*, that is available on Amazon as paperback or ebook. He's had an article on the Titanic published in a literary anthology called *Watermarks*, in aid of the Calder Valley Flood Relief Charity, and an article he wrote—using the pseudonym Albert Hall—about J.G. Ballard has been published on the cultural literary website www.literaryyard.com.

He won second prize in the Pen Nib International Writing Competition 2021 for his essay *Who Guards the Guardians* (about the unacknowledged power of the press and the media). His comic one act play, *Elvis and the Psychiatrist*, has been shown at the Sundance ten minute comedy festival at the Sixth Theatre in Racine, Wisconsin. Another one act drama, *A Restive Audience*, has been published in *Hello Godot! An Anthology of One Act Plays, Volume 2* by Fresh Words publishing company in

America; and another play, *The Conference Speech*, has been published in another anthology by the same company.

He also enjoys painting, drawing and photography.

- https://discriminatingthoughts.wordpress.com/
- X (formerly Twitter): @readyverbiage

Susan Temple

Susan contributed and was published in the book *The Art of Wild Swimming* (2021) and her short story *Life Preserver* won an award at *The 2023 Scotland's Indie Book Festival*. She is currently working on her debut psychological thriller novel entitled *Stranded on Stroma*.

When not writing Susan enjoys fundraising for causes close to her heart and has taken part in running, canoeing, abseiling and skydiving challenges.

Susan lives in Caithness, Scotland with her husband and two children.

Jim Gilbert

Jim has been 'dabbling' in writing for a number of years now. He recently decided to take it more seriously and created his *Quick Bite Horror* series. The aim is to create short horror story collections that can be read in those short gaps that life gives us, be it waiting for a bus or a doctor's appointment etc. There are three QBH collections available as well as *Revenant*—a stand alone novella, all available on kindle or paperback, with more on the way.

Jim has some novels in progress too, so plenty for all horror fans to get their teeth into!

- Facebook: https://www.facebook.com/quickbitehorror/
- Instagram: @quickbitehorror
- X (formerly Twitter): @j1mg1lbert

WR James

WR James is a technical author by profession but has always written fiction, including novels, short stories and flash fiction. He has self-published several collections on Amazon including *Christmas Evils* 1 & 2 and *When The Screaming Starts*. Currently he is working on his third novel, *The Crime*, and his third collection of Christmas horror stories, *Christmas Evils* 3. He lives with his wife in the Norfolk Broads National Park, England and enjoys reading, music and walking.

- https://www.amazon.co.uk/dp/B0BJDP52BG
- Facebook: https://www.facebook.com/profile.php?id=100091365961985

Robin Kilmister

Robin Kilmister is a filmwriting graduate hailing from Oxfordshire in the UK. He currently writes short stories as a hobby with plans to publish more frequently. He can be found on most social networks including Instagram and X.

- https://robinkilmister.com/
- Instagram: @the_kilmister
- X (formerly Twitter): @Honourable_Fish

David Maguire

David Maguire is a UK-based writer, script editor, podcast host and former film festival programmer. He is the author of the Columbia University Press book on the film *I Spit On Your Grave*, and has spoken at various conferences across the UK on topics as varied as the Final Girl and Women in Horror, the rape-revenge genre, monstrous femininity in 21st century film and George A. Romero's zombie films as neo-Westerns.

- LinkedIn: https://www.linkedin.com/in/david-maguire-86b799254/
- Instagram: @ispitonyourdave
- X (formerly Twitter): @ispitonyourdave

Matthew Tett

Matthew Tett is a freelance writer living in Wiltshire. He has been published in *Writing in Education*, the *Cardiff Review*, the *New Welsh Review*, and *Ink Sweat and Tears*. His short story *Spun Sugar* was published in the inaugural edition of *Liberally*. In 2021, he won Word After Word's mini memoir prize. Matthew is a reader for the Edinburgh Flash Fiction and Short Story prizes and a developmental editor for *Flash Fiction Magazine*. He is also the producer of *StoryTown*.

- Instagram: @CreativeInBoA
- X (formerly Twitter): @CountryBoyWales

Kenneth Walker

Kenneth has been writing all his life, he has submitted several short stories to different contests. he has done freelance work writing articles for newspapers and for a company creating an RPG.

Ivan Richardson

Born in Scotland, Ivan Richardson studied Mechanical Engineering at Leicester University (UK). Ivan is also a member of Leicester Writers club, which helped him perfect his writing skills. His other hobbies include martial arts where he holds a fourth degree black belt in Tae Kwon do.

- Amazon UK: https://www.amazon.co.uk/~/e/Bo9SVFJ8K8
- ISFDB: https://www.isfdb.org/cgi-bin/ea.cgi?333529
- X (formerly Twitter): @IvanRic19103369

Barlow Crassmont

Barlow is an English teacher who writes poetry and short fiction stories in his spare time. His work has been published online by Free Flash Fiction, The Chamber Magazine, and Wilderness House Literary Review; and in print, in the literary journal *The Other Side of Hope*.

- X (formerly Twitter): @barlowcrassmont

Callum Melvein

Callum is a young and talented writer who is supported at Buzz Hub St Helens CDP. This is a day service that provides activities and opportunities for adults with learning difficulties and/or autism. Callum is a budding author and he writes short stories and poetry whenever he can. St Helens CDP supported Callum in the self-publishing of his first children's book, however his favourite genre remains to be horror and thriller.

In his own words: 'It was always my dream to create stories for people and to be an author.'

- https://sthelenscdp.co.uk/
- Facebook: https://www.facebook.com/BuzzHubStHelenscdp/
- Instagram: @buzzhubsthelenscdp

The Attic Room

C.S. Dines

I loved that attic room from the off.

And despite the subsequent events I'm about to describe, there remains *some* small fondness for it still ...

***

England, the very early nineties, and the start of my final year as an undergraduate in an all-male household of five. Ahead on the glimmering grown-up horizon our glorious futures beckoned. Although whether such was likely remained to be seen; whatever spiel we'd been fed about how obtaining a degree was a ticket to the big time, the approaching recession suggested we'd been sold a pup. It was becoming increasingly clear that proceeding through higher education wasn't about to be readily reciprocated by a booming job market—Blair's *Cool Britannia* was still a few years away yet.

Not that this initially mattered. I had months before I needed to worry about all that. For now, I was simply up for making the most of this last stretch of student life.

My four housemates and I hailed from all over the country (Essex in my case). We'd initially been shoved together as campus flatmates during Freshers' Week, and had stuck out each other's company in two further houses for the duration of our three year 'sojourn' in that windy, northern English city.

How did we manage to stay together for so long? I think our dynamic worked because by some lucky quirk of fate we were all similar enough to get on extremely well but individual enough not to crowd each other. Which proved essential in preventing familiarity from breeding any lasting contempt.

Who'd got what room in our *first* house had been handled democratically by randomly selecting numbers from a badly scratched saucepan. And so for my sophomore year, I'd occupied what was by far the smallest room in a two storey corner terrace found at the bottom end of a busy main road, opposite an all-night petrol station.

On balance it wasn't uncomfortable. But after accounting for a desk, single bed and wardrobe, even the proverbial swinging cat would've found things pretty tight—basically the landlord had split a much larger room unevenly in half for additional rent.

We decided to move again in our third and final year because for most students this was very much the done thing. We also wanted to be a bit closer to campus—I guess we probably had at least half an eye on exam finals and making life easy on ourselves.

Given most rentable accommodation available comprised of more virtually interchangeable red bricked terraces set within mazes of narrow streets that had varying levels of incline, we weren't exactly spoilt for choice.

But after a week-long search prior to the summer break, we did find one such house which earned collective approval. And in the spirit of that great British sense of fair play, I was allowed to take first pick of the new rooms to compensate for my previous year's 'sacrifice'.

The rest were decided by a different saucepan ...

***

The coolest thing about that attic room was the skylight. It instantly drew your eye when you walked in, and that's what clinched the deal for me.

Being up top I was further away from everyone else: a whole extra creaky staircase away in fact—a little winding one that had been latterly added through renovation, and led you up to barely a landing, and the recently added room beyond.

Despite my 5'11 height, the slanted part of the off-white ceiling, within which the skylight was centred, posed less of a hazard to my forehead than it otherwise might have. For orientation's sake I faced the back of the house. Down below, a flimsy back door in the galley kitchen led out to a small yard, mainly for the bins, and an even narrower street running behind.

A more contemporary feature, the skylight itself was double glazed, unlike the traditional sash windows on the other levels, and was held fast in a sturdy brown wooden frame: there was no additional blind. It was very easy to operate. Not that I ever opened it much. Like I said, it was a windy city.

Allowing for the slant, the room—which one entered via the nearside bottom corner—was otherwise rectangular. Instead of getting all technical I'd say it was one and a half rungs up from 'cosy' which—considering my last room was borderline to one rung down—was definitely an improvement!

Wall décor was a fading blue complemented by a darker carpet somewhat in need of CPR. In the other bottom corner, running lengthways towards the skylight end, was a decent enough bed, single again but with useful drawers underneath. Facing it was a small but really cool looking black bookshelf, that had been leant just below where the ceiling's gradient eventually met the wall. Back on the nearside, a rusting but functional two bar electric heater rested against the wall halfway between the door and the top of bed (there were no radiators anywhere in the house).

The *pièce de résistance* however was the desk. Don't get me wrong, I mean it was just an ordinary writing desk, and in considerable need of a good dusting. But what made it special was how it stood directly under the skylight. I could see myself sat there scribbling away at some great literary masterpiece in the wee small hours, while a beaming full moon peered in from that skylight right above my head. It couldn't have looked more appropriate if it tried.

Such were the pretentions of a skinny twenty-year old now on the home straight of his English degree …

***

Once we actually moved in, a dull weekend in early September, I quickly got to work in bringing my new quarters to life.

The black bookshelf (which I always had to kneel down to get at) was spot on for my required classics, plus it had extra space for any recreational reading should I seek to be enigmatically alone on a rainy afternoon. I also added my own portable shelving (which I'd brought up from home), to run in parallel to the bed along the nearside wall. This was mainly for a few more books, and my CDs, cassettes and music system —there was no such thing as Spotify yet! Meanwhile, I stuck a much smaller bedside table in between the heater and the headboard, which was for my faithful silver clock radio/reading light combi, as well as my current book at bedtime.

One thing this attic room didn't have however was a wardrobe. Although, those bed drawers at least solved the underwear and socks storage issue, with enough to spare for other minor essentials too. Luckily, that previous summer my dad had insightfully purchased for me a stylish metal clothes rack that, once I painstakingly fitted it together, I was just about able to run along the same wall as the additional shelf before the ceiling's slant intervened; I piled a couple of smaller boxes and cases in the remaining corner next to it.

The rack wasn't quite able to carry every item of clothing though so here's where things got really innovative. Despite having already put up a few pictures and posters—favourite bands, favourite cult movies: nearly everybody had that *Betty Blue* one pasted up back then—I still had enough space across the three taller walls (not the skylight end obviously) to bang in a smattering of strong nails. Upon each I was able to balance a coat hanger where I could display my fancier jackets or paisley waistcoats—waistcoats were really in at that time, as were ponytails, and my everyday appearance was modelled more on some kind of urbane poet look, rather than grungy stude.

Finally, it just remained for me to make the desk functional. And add my preferred seat, which was a black director's style chair complete with my name—ALEX DAY—in white block capitals on the back of it.

Et voilà!

I've always been the more obsessive type who won't usually rest until everything looks as it should. So while my housemates merely dumped most of their stuff and then reasoned it was time for tea, I didn't appear until everything in my attic room was just so ...

***

The night it all happened was less than a week before our finals were due to start.

I'd been sat at my desk until well past midnight. I should have been studying. But, as I've already indicated, I had other aspirations, so instead I'd been writing something I hoped was hugely profound (but more likely profoundly ridiculous) in a favoured A4 sized black notebook I'd reserved for this sort of melancholia.

It was a clear night, so the moon was aptly visible in the skylight above, although my desk lamp was the one providing much needed illumination. The rest of my room meanwhile was daubed in apposite ethereal shadow.

In years gone by I'd have found that creepy: all alone at the very top of an old terraced house with its various random creaks long after baleful distant chimes marking the witching hour had ceased: how much more classic horror movie vibe could you get? But I'd long grown out of such irrationality. Now I didn't mind the dark: I hardly ever put the main bedroom light on, preferring this softer, more atmospheric setting instead. Besides, wasn't this the preferred mood music for any tortured literary genius—although some of my housemates often called me a vampire, given I would often still be up gone silly o'clock too.

Even vampires need to sleep though. So it was just approaching one o'clock when I finally crawled into my own coffin, after having shut the bedroom door and switched off the lamp to let some early summer moonlight take over.

I didn't drift off instantly. Instead I vaguely remember staring absently at the skylight as my eyes adjusted to the darkness, lost in thought about what I was trying to write, and how to improve it.

I couldn't have been lying there for more than five minutes when I heard some noise coming from the smaller street behind our house.

I say noise; what I actually heard sounded like a big crowd of people outside. A whole army of god knows who had abruptly appeared from wherever, and they were hollering their heads off as they made their way along.

Given I was still wide awake this didn't particularly bother me despite the ungodly hour. That couldn't necessarily be said for the rest of my housemates however, or our neighbours.

The closer this group got, the louder they got. I had no idea what they were shouting. They certainly weren't singing or chanting though, as might be more customary for drunken revellers returning home. They sounded ... *angrier*? I could tell there were an awful lot of them too: perhaps a whole crowd of football supporters' worth. However, they seemed far too incensed for even the most vociferous footie fans. Bizarrely, I envisioned a mob of furious villagers brandishing burning torches and pitchforks as they marched towards Dracula's or Victor Frankenstein's Castle.

Maybe they're after the vampire at number ten, I joked to myself as they got ever closer.

Just as they appeared to reach our yard, something switched which completely threw me. I don't know how, but suddenly all those unintelligible cries were literally in my room! The row was almost deafening, and I noticed it was now accompanied by some really fast, heavy thumping too, as if people were also pounding on something very solid.

ThumpThumpThumpThump!

What the f— was going on?! I was so disoriented it took quite a few seconds before I realised, more to my bewilderment than horror, these sounds were now actually coming from the walls!

The whole thing was so impossibly crazy: was a baying mob really trapped *inside* them?

Seriously?!

Even as the raging cries and hammering intensified, a removed and distinctly calm voice within me reasoned, *Alex mate, you've finally gone mad.*

There could be no other explanation: I was hearing things; I'd flipped!

So this is what it's like to lose your mind. My future was to be padded cells and straightjackets. To be honest, that prospect was way more frightening than what was supposedly going on all around me.

The whole disturbance lasted about two more minutes before reaching a natural jarring crescendo. Then, it slowly faded away like the diminishing climactic wail of some tuneless heavy metal track.

I remained in a state of high alert, and hadn't moved a muscle throughout, but I also welcomed the respite now it was all over.

Only it wasn't.

I was very, *very* wrong about that...

***

You know, I still physically shiver from the same palpable chill I felt the second I saw it.

Up until that point my gaze had been fixed to the wall nearest my bed while that entire unworldly cacophony played itself out. But, when I turned to look at the ceiling, I audibly gasped and my heart must have dropped three beats from utter shock.

Darkness: *total* darkness! It was as if a giant, pulsating sphere of impenetrable pitch black energy had materialised right over my head. It wasn't doing anything either ... it was just sitting there; just *waiting*.

I was absolutely petrified. I may not have been visited by a ghastly, spectral figure or howling shade, but I instantly sensed something a great deal more terrifying had arrived in my room instead: pure evil incarnate!

I don't know how I knew that. Even now, I can only infer a kind of visceral cognisance had drawn this awful conclusion. Far worse, this same heightened intuition also knew exactly what *It* was waiting for, what *It* wanted.

Me!

Utter icy dread, worse than my very worst childhood nightmares—the ones so truly monstrous you couldn't even scream—overpowered me. Those nightmares were now here, wrapped inside this malevolent presence in my attic room.

They'd come to get me: *Evil* itself had come to get me!

I didn't debate. I didn't hypothesise on what I did or didn't believe in. Struggling for both breath and voice against fear unlike anything I'd ever experienced, I forced my eyes to close as tight as they bloody well could, blocking out this predacious ball of 'unlight'. Then, I did something I hadn't done since school assembly.

I started praying!

Why? Because my conviction held that if some demonic entity from Hell itself truly had come for me, then conversely only divine intervention could literally save my soul.

I mentally floundered for the *Lord's Prayer* as my incantation of choice for a desperate, makeshift exorcism—I didn't know any others!

With my eyelids still clamped shut, I began to intone in urgent stilted whispers.

'Our father ...'

Please God make this work!

'Who art in heaven ...'

It's still there; I know it's still there!

'Hallowed be thy name ...'

Go away! Go away! Go away!

'Thy kingdom come ...'

Jesus Christ help me!

'Thy will be done ...'

It's not working! Oh shit! Oh shit! Oh f—!

'On Earth as it is in Heaven ...'

What's it going to do to me?!

I think it was only when I'd got as far as, 'For thine is the glory ...', that at last I perceived something *had* changed, lifted.

Cautiously I opened my eyes.

Halle-effing-lujah!

I was right. *It* had completely, and thankfully, vanished.

While the remaining shadows slipped back to their more usual positions around a once again moonlit room, my heart took forever to stop thumping as hard as those walls had seemingly been earlier. I still hadn't moved. My nerves were both shredded and shot to bits. I kept exhaling in a swift succession of relieved and eternally grateful gasps. I just couldn't stop staring at the ceiling either, unable to fully banish the sinister image of what I was *so* sure had been there moments before.

I really don't know how long it was until I at last dared myself to jump out of bed and switch on the main light, ritualistically burning away every last vestige of lingering gloom.

It stayed on for the rest of the night ...

***

There isn't much to add.

The next morning, I was naturally up before the others (I hadn't slept a wink), but I purposely stayed quiet to see if any of them mentioned anything about hearing a murderous racket outside the previous night: nobody ever did.

Outwardly, I pretended that everything was normal. Inwardly, I simply couldn't put what I'd seen out of my mind. That thing, whatever *It* had been, wanted me.

I kept to the lounge or kitchen all day. I really needed the inconsequentially loud chatter of the telly or the reassuring sight of my housemates close by. Only after everyone else had, at various intervals, disappeared for the night did I cautiously venture back up to my room.

I didn't sleep that night either. With lights blazing I just stared at the ceiling again, dreading *Its* return.

This continued for the remaining weeks of that last summer term. I looked well beyond tired, and consequently struggled to concentrate during my finals.

I also stopped writing at my desk. Fact was how could I sit there all alone without having an eerie feeling there was *something* behind me?

Nothing did ever happen again though; and it's been about thirty years since! Nonetheless, there's been a lasting effect: I'm almost always on edge once the sun goes down.

You see, I can still hear those cries beyond the skylight of my super cool attic room coming down the road towards me; I can still hear them screaming in the walls!

And I simply can't shake a cold certainty that evil—for I'm certain it is *Evil*—is still somewhere in the darkness, waiting for me.

But I have my prayers, and I keep the lights on ...

Silver Roses

Poppy Whitworth

Gabby loved wandering around the car boot sales on a Sunday morning, finding long lost treasures and antiques. She laid out today's haul on the table, flicked the kettle on and made herself a sweet cup of tea

She was pleased with the items she had dug out of boxes and plastic containers. A glass vase, a dainty pair of teacups with matching saucers, a knitted Scandinavian style cardigan and some beaded jewellery. But her favourite find of the day was a silver photo frame. The frame held an old sepia photo of a Victorian child. Or was it a doll? Gabby couldn't quite tell, but it didn't matter, she would chuck that away. It was the frame covered in silver roses entwined together that she wanted.

After her tea, she found a place for all her new things. She filled her vase with flowers from the garden and placed it on the kitchen table. The cups and saucers were carefully tucked away in a cupboard with the rest of the mismatched sets, whilst the cardigan and beads were placed in her wardrobe. The frame was given a special place to rest and sat proudly on the mantel above the fireplace.

She discarded the picture and replaced it with a photo of her mum, who had passed almost twelve years ago. Gabby smiled, kissed her fingers and touched the picture.

'Love you mum,' she whispered. It was the only good picture she had of her, and it deserved to be displayed beautifully.

It was mid-October, and the dark, cold nights were creeping in. She found it especially lonely this time of year and longed to meet someone who she could share a bottle of wine and a warm blanket with.

That night like every night, Gabby went to bed wearing thick pyjamas and cuddling a hot water bottle. Living in an old cottage, the windows were low to the floor and she liked to have the curtains open and watch the night come alive. She would lie there watching the car lights whizz past like shooting stars, sometimes a stray cat would meander by in search of a late-night snack. Streetlamps acted like spotlights on a stage, illuminating late night walkers who perhaps wanted to go by unseen.

Gabby shuffled in bed, changing her position, when she spotted something on the floor. She swung her legs out, reached down and picked it up. It was the photo from the frame. How did that get there? She was sure she had thrown it out. She studied the image for a while. The girl must have been around the age of fourteen. Her hair hung in dark loose ringlets past her shoulders with a bow pinning up one side. Her facial expression was neutral so she couldn't detect how the girl was feeling and she wore what Gabby could only assume was a white Victorian dress. There was something off about the image though, it was the eyes, they were glazed over, devoid of life. She shuddered and ripped the photo into pieces and put it on the bedside table ready to be tossed in the bin the next morning. She wrapped herself up a little bit more tightly that night before drifting off to sleep.

Gabby woke to a dull, gloomy morning, the sky was grey and promised rain. She groaned, knowing she would get soaked on her commute to work. She stretched and locked eyes on the photograph. It was propped up against her lamp untorn and unmarked. Gabby's hand shook as she reached out for the picture. Disbelief filled her mind, yet she knew clearly she tore it up. It was now perfectly intact, except something had changed? The girl's face was contorted into a frown, like she was angry about something. Gabby's phone buzzed, pulling her back into reality. Glancing at the clock she swore under her breath as she realised she was running late.

Gabby forgot all about the photo that was left lying on the sofa, where she had flung it as she raced out the door. She arrived at work late, soaking wet and cold, and her boss greeted her with a stern telling off. She spent the whole day chilly and damp and to top it off she forgot to bring her lunch. By the time she arrived home she was irritated and hungry.

Gabby banged around the kitchen, throwing open the oven door and shoving in a lasagne to heat up, then marched upstairs to change. She plated up her dinner and poured herself a generous glass of red wine. She went through to the lounge and lit the wood burner, listening as it crackled into life. She was about to sit down when she saw the photograph waiting for her. Turning it over, she noticed looped handwriting on the back.

'Rose Attwood, B.1847 D.1861.'

'Sorry Rose, but I've had enough for today,' Gabby said as she tossed the picture into the fire, where it dissolved into the blaze.

Eventually feeling warm and full she finally began to relax and feel like herself again. With the monotonous sound of the tv and the flickering of the flames she soon fell asleep.

Gabby woke engulfed by the dark with only a single flame casting a glow around the room. It was late and she needed to get to bed. She walked over to the frame to say goodnight to her mum. But in the centre of the silver roses was the picture of the Victorian girl.

Bile filled her mouth as she looked into the fireplace. That single flame consumed her favourite photo of her mum until there was nothing left. Cold, angry tears formed in her eyes as she flung the frame against the wall. The glass shattered into pieces.

Gabby went up to bed knowing her mum's picture couldn't replace the real thing, yet she felt the loss of it weigh heavy on her heart. In her grief she didn't take the time to wonder why or how her mum's image ended up as ashes, whilst Rose remained untouched and unscathed.

She woke at three AM with a sharp pain in her left shoulder blade. Gasping, she ran to the bathroom to look in the mirror.

There, embedded in her flesh was a large shard of glass. She could hear a faint malicious laugh echo all around her, and she knew it was Rose.

Blood trickled down her back as she pulled the fragment out. Her eyes watered with the pain as she pressed a towel over the wound to stem the flow of blood. Eventually she dressed and took the piece downstairs with her.

Fear crept over her as she approached the frame on the floor. The glass within was somehow put back together except for one single segment. The bloody fragment was like a missing puzzle piece that slotted in perfectly. Roses face, now smeared with Gabby's blood held an unnatural and evil smile.

Gabby snatched up the frame and her keys and left the cottage. She walked amongst the shadows until she reached the graveyard. It was still and quiet amongst the graves. Feeling like the dead belonged with their own kind, she placed the photo under a large oak tree surrounded by withered brown leaves.

'You can rest now, Rose,' Gabby whispered into the night.

The wind sighed in response, and she knew she had done the right thing.

It was years later that she finally had the courage to research the photograph. She learnt that Rose's untimely death was caused by scarlet fever. She also discovered that post-mortem photography was popular during Victorian times. Taking photos of the deceased was a way of preserving the memory of a loved one.

Gabby was never haunted by Rose again, but the jagged edge of skin on her shoulder served as a reminder that some things belong to the dead.

The Head Gardner

Masimba Musodza

The furious banging on the door shattered his dream. Shaun sat up with a start, the bed groaning loudly like a sated hippopotamus, precluding the possibility that he could pretend to whoever it was at the main door that he wasn't home. It was too early for the knocking to be an Amazon delivery. Shaun wasn't expecting one, but the people in the two flats upstairs got those nearly every day. Sometimes, if the banging persisted, they would come down and answer the door themselves.

It was the police. Two young ladies in their early twenties, business-like in their demeanour.

'Good morning, sir. I am WPC Haleema Khan, and my colleague is WPC Grace Maitland. We would like a word with Mr Shaun Wilde, a gentleman we believe to reside at this address. Is he in?'

Shaun nodded absently, then realised he had to be verbal about his communication. 'I'm Shaun. I don't know about the gentleman part, so you might be looking for someone else, actually.'

The cops did not join him in his laughter, and he broke it off with an awkward cough.

'Two nights ago, you were picked up along the A19 by a group of friends in a van,' said WPC Khan.

'Yes, uni students,' said Shaun. 'I can't recall all their names, but I think the driver was called Mordecai, and his girlfriend Mikaela.'

'Mordecai Knight, aged 21,' said WPC Maitland, consulting her notebook, 'and Mikaela Jackson, also 21. The other passengers were Wendy Little, 20, James Chen, 21 and Izzy McLaren, 22.'

'Has anything happened to them?' Shaun asked. He could have kicked himself for blurting out the question his inner voice had just told him not to. There was something incriminating about such a question at this point in time.

'That is what we'd like to know, and we thought you could be of some help, sir,' said WPC Khan. 'You see, all five students have been reported missing. We know they picked you up on the A19, near Middlesbrough. They were on their way to Newcastle, but the last image of their van is a few miles near the Little Thorpe junction. It looks like you were the last person to see all five.'

'Five? What about the gardener?' Shaun asked.

The cops exchanged glances.

'Yeah, a lass,' said Shaun. 'We picked her up on the A19 as well, about two minutes after Billingham. She said she was the head gardener at a house, some fancy name. She was in the van when they dropped me at Peterlee.'

'And you don't remember this gardener's name at all, sir?' said WPC Maitland.

Shaun shook his head. 'I only recall the driver's name because it is not very common, and his girlfriend's because I have a sister also called Mikaela.' He knew what this looked like. Too much information, none of it useful, too readily given. Their faces said it all.

Suddenly, he remembered her name. 'Hedwig!' he said with alacrity, startling the two officers. 'That's what the gardener said her name was, it's just come back to me now.'

'Hedwig, like in *Harry Potter*?' WPC Khan asked.

'No, Hedwig Gardner.'

They stared blankly at him.

'She said people called her Hed Gardner, because she was head gardener at this place. Get it, head gardener ...' His forced laugh was met by blank stares, and died away. 'It was funny when she said it in the van. Wendy said all her life she had lived with jokes about her Little Wendy House ...'

Humour was wasted on these cops, Shaun thought, dismissing them with a wave of his hand. There was also the uneasy realisation that the reason he wasn't tickling their funny bone was because they had already decided he was guilty of whatever they had come to see him about.

'Sir, do you mind making a statement about the events during the time you were in the company of these missing persons, up to when they dropped you off?' said WPC Khan. 'A description of this previously unknown passenger, Hedwig Gardner, would also be appreciated.'

Shaun sighed. At least they were not asking him to accompany them back to the station. More importantly, Shaun felt he was more articulate as a writer than a speaker. He stepped aside from the doorway. 'You better come in, then, officers,' he said. This time, he did not smile.

Two nights ago, Shaun was walking home from rehearsals in Stockton-on-Tees. It was warm, and he wasn't in a particular rush to get home. What's more, he could save that two pounds for a good rummaging on the 'reduced price' shelf at the shops. If he got to Middlesbrough on time, he reminded himself, and upped his pace. He should have just accepted that lift from Lana. Ignored how small he felt ensconced in the passenger seat, next to one of the most beautiful and unobtainable women he had seen in years, while she made plans for the rest of the night over the phone with men more in her league.

This part was not going into his statement, of course, but it made Shaun pause and look pensively at the blank wall ahead before he forced himself back to the task at hand. As he approached the Iron Bridge, Sabrina, his cousin, had called. She had been asked to fill in at the warehouse where she worked; could he come over and mind the kids right away?

That is how Shaun had found himself running along the A19, hoping to reach the next bus stop before the X10 to Newcastle via Peterlee, that had already left Middlesbrough Bus Station, reached the highway. He inserted Sabrina's number in the statement, suppressing with a sharp effort that recurring reminder that he was being overly generous with the details.

A white van had pulled up in front of him. As he passed it, a friendly face, Mikaela Jackson, had popped out of the passenger's window and invited him to hop in. That is how he had met the university students. Conversation was casual. They were impressed to learn that he had been a successful TV actor in the early 2000s. One of the students was studying film making, so they swapped numbers.

They picked up Hedwig Gardner just outside Billingham. Long dark hair, piercing green eyes, slightly upturned nose, one crooked tooth, slim built, probably in her early thirties. Even as he wrote this down, that feeling he was delivering way too much information for someone who did not know what happened to the missing students returned. He was thinking of the police procedural drama he had been in all those years ago.

Hedwig was on her way to a fancy-name house, where she worked as the head gardener. She had smiled and nodded good-naturedly at the laughter her name and job description drew. The film student had proposed she capitalise on the pun to become a celebrity gardener, so they swapped numbers. Shaun had dropped off at the roundabout turn-off at Peterlee. That was the last he had seen of everyone who had been on that van.

The two policewomen had thanked him for his statement, and said they would be in touch if they had any more questions. Shaun doubted they would, but he was sure they would keep a close eye on him and delve into his digital footprint. They would find nothing linking him to the students, or Hedwig Gardner. He hoped the students were alright. They had been a right canny bunch.

As for Hedwig, if he was honest to himself, there was something about her that had left a lasting impression. The startlingly green eyes, her half-smile that hid her crooked tooth, when he corrected one of the students who said Hedwig had a Geordie accent. In fact, she had a Mackem accent. Knowing this difference between the dialect spoken in Newcastle from that in Sunderland had not only broken the ice, but set him apart from the other people in the van.

Except, Shaun had not indicated further interest. He knew he should have. The same way he knew he should have indicated his interest in Lana the first time they met and she had been impressed with his career. If only he could overcome the feeling of inadequacy that had engulfed him since Paloma had walked out on him. Just yesterday, he had seen her in *Es-*

quire, those eyes that had once adored him, but had grown to despise him soon after his agent dropped him, staring at an ornate bottle of perfume in her hand.

His mobile phone rang, snatching him from his despondent musing. The number was not on his contacts list. Yet, he had a feeling it was not a debt collector. He tapped the green icon with his index.

'Hi, Shaun!' a familiar voice greeted him cheerfully. He groped for a name.

'Hi, er ...'

'It's Hedwig! Remember, Hedwig Gardner, the Head Gardener ...'

Shaun heard his heart pound and his blood race in his ears. 'Hed wig!' he said, through laboured breath. He tried to remember giving her his number. 'I never thought I'd hear from you again.'

'A'way, Shaun, don't give up so easily!' she said, and laughed.

'I wasn't aware I was even in pursuit,' he said. But, the shock and fright were giving way to a growing desire.

'Well, you are, pet!' she said. 'Think whatever you like of me, but I am not going to play too hard to get.'

There was a long pause. 'I don't know what to say, Hedwig.'

'Say you'll come see me tonight, Shaun.'

'See you where?'

'I told you I am the head gardener at Griddlesfield Hall, near Murton,' said Hedwig, impatiently. 'You can take the train to Seaham and get a taxi. I knock off at five, I have a cottage behind the main house. A'way, man, don't make a lass beg!'

The confidence of the old Shaun coursed through him. 'OK, Hedwig, I'll give you a ring when I am in Seaham,' he said. 'I'll be a bit late, though. I have rehearsals in Stockton for this movie, then I am all yours.'

He hung up as she uttered a squeal of delight. Shaun stood in the middle of the room, the mobile phone still inches from his face, and had a *what's just happened?!* moment. It's not as if he'd never had a woman throw herself at him, he reminded himself. Back in the day, when he was a regular feature on television, it went with the territory. With this movie, and the one he was writing, perhaps the good old days were coming back. Why, he might even take a chance on Lana?

Chuckling to himself, all doubt and apprehension dispelled from his mind, Shaun went to the kitchen to make himself some breakfast.

He got off the train at Seaham station at around nine. The sun had just set. Live music blared from the social club nearby, but the street outside the station was empty. Three taxis waited. Shaun jumped into the first one. The driver, a portly, middle-aged man of South Asian appearance, grinned at him in the rear-view mirror as he started the vehicle. 'Where to, boss?' he asked.

'Griddlesfield Hall, mate,' said Shaun.

'What's the postcode?'

'Postcode?' Shaun whipped out his phone. 'Just a second boss, let me check my phone.' He rang Hedwig. She picked up immediately. 'Babe, I'm in the taxi, and the driver needs the postcode.' *Babe?*

'I don't know the postcode,' said Hedwig. 'I don't get any mail. Look, tell him it's Griddlesfield Hall, it's a landmark around here.'

'Do you know where Griddlesfield Hall is, mate?' said Shaun to the driver.

'Sorry, mate, no,' said the driver. 'I need the postcode to feed into the app.' He indicated to the mobile phone on dashboard.

'OK, tell him to take you to the Boar's Head, an old pub. It's within walking distance of my place, I will meet you there.'

Shaun relayed the information to the driver. Muttering to himself, he relayed it to his map. 'Ah!' he said, pleased with the results. 'It's just outside Murton.' He began to pull out of the station car park.

Shaun sank back, and thought about the immediate future with a dreamy smile on his face. The director had complimented him on his performance during the rehearsals. Earlier, he had managed to do twenty pages of the screenplay. It really seemed as if his life was lifting from the doldrums.

'Have they reopened the hospital?'

The question snatched him out of his reverie. 'Hmm?'

'The hospital near the pub, or a mental home,' said the driver. 'We used to pick up a lot of people who worked there in the winter, when they couldn't walk to and from the train station. The stories they had! It was a dangerous place, sort of like a prison for people who couldn't go to prison but couldn't be allowed back into the community either. I heard it was shut during the Lockdown.'

'I don't know anything about a hospital,' said Shaun. 'I'm going to see my new lass.'

'Oh.' The driver's grin was knowing and conspiratorial, but there were creases on his forehead. 'Look, we're here, mate.'

As the taxi pulled up, Shaun could make out the ruins of a boarded up pub, surrounded by open country. He hoped there were no dog walkers about. This far from residential areas, they often let their dogs wander, with no regard for the invisible disabilities of this world, such as cynophobia.

As the taxi drove off, utter silence descended. Shaun strained his ears, frantically hoping to hear at least the wind. And, even though there was no wind, a chill gripped his bones.

'Oh, Shaun, you came!'

Shaun nearly screamed as Hedwig emerged from the shadow of the Boar's Head. She wore a dark T-shirt and leggings. He had half-expected her to dress up, but he wasn't too disappointed. Her eyes pierced the gloom, and her breath was warm on his face before their lips locked.

'Come on, the house is just there, behind those trees,' she said as she released him. 'My cottage is just behind it.'

Shaun looked across the street, and made out the rooftop above the trees. He let her lead him.

'You live in the middle of nowhere,' he said.

'Are you crazy, Shaun?' she said, laughing. 'You could jog over to Murton for a pint of milk and be back before the kettle's boiled, you know.'

Shaun glanced around, and all he saw was the countryside. The heavy silence was disturbing. He tried to shut it out of his awareness. They were walking down a path in the clump of trees, the first evidence of human settlement since they had left the pub. Hedwig was walking ahead, her shadow swung slowly across the bushes like a black searchlight.

'Hedwig, the police came to see me this morning,' said Shaun. His head thudded in his ears. 'Remember those students in the van, the night we met?' She seemed to have quickened her pace, she was a lot further from him now, but she turned to face him, a pale blur in the dark. 'Seems they have not been seen since that night. The police thought I was the last person to see them, but it looks like the last person was, in fact, you, babe.'

Babe?

Hedwig seemed to be waiting for him to catch up. As he neared her, eyes caught the stars above. That sense that something was wrong lingered. He took another step forward. He yelped as his foot plunged into a void, then the rest of his body followed. He banged his head against the rim of the hole. Hot crimson splashed down his face in spurts. He felt his consciousness ebb.

The next thing he knew, he was bathed in the brilliant grey of a full moon. There was an overpowering smell of compost, and rotting meat. Shaun tried to move, but his whole body from the neck downwards was in a tight grip. Frantically, he jerked this way and that, his grunts rising to screams that carried into the still of the night. Tears of utter frustration surged, stinging the wounds on his face. He remembered the fall, the bump on his head. Perhaps he had broken his spine, too, and was now paralysed.

If that was the case, then how come he could feel the constriction on his chest, and the rocks digging into different parts of his body? Realisation dawned on him in a wave of horror; from the neck down, Shaun was buried in the ground.

As he opened his mouth to scream again, the football sized mound about two feet from his face moved almost imperceptibly. It was another head! He glanced around, there were at least six heads in his field of vision. Most lolled to one side at odd angles, but one turned slowly to gaze at him blindly out of eyes like burst, decaying fruit, a dark fluid seeping from one of them, down a battered face. Swollen lips quavered to form words, but could only manage a series of sobs and moans.

Shaun recognised him by his moustache. The student film maker from the van! Shaun had given him his number. That is how Hedwig had obtained it. Hedwig ...

She was standing over him, blotting the light of the moon. Those piercing green eyes seemed dull now. She leaned against the shaft of a gardening implement, maybe a hoe.

'Hedwig!' said Shaun, through gasps. 'What the hell is going on?'

'I told you I was the head gardener, didn't I, Shaun?' she said, her voice level. 'Now, I need to get a bed ready for the taxi driver who brought you in earlier this evening. I'll be back to have a look at you in the morning.'

She walked away. Soon, he heard the rhythmic thud of the earth being dug into. He heard it for a long time. Then, he slipped back into unconsciousness.

The Reflection In My Soul

Elizabeth Butler

The mirror showed a reflection that wasn't my own. When I stared directly at the misty image, where there should have been myself staring back, a wolf's head had taken its place.

Its ashy grey fur swayed with no breeze. Its eyes dark like the bottom of an abyss. The creature was large, but stood upright like a human, wearing the same clothes as I had. Ripped jeans and a torn white t shirt I'd bought in the sale. Whenever I would cock my head to the side, trying to remove my long, tangled hair from my eyes, this creature would copy me.

Other people may have been terrified by this prospect, but somehow, I was intrigued. I was lost inside its thoughts, my pupils transfixed on its fur, blowing in the wind from across a different universe.

The alarm on my phone vibrated inside my pocket, making me snap out of my trance. My eyes started to adjust to the bright screen, glaring in front of me, coming to terms with what I was seeing. The time 7:45 AM flashing and drowning out my current thoughts. When I glanced back at the old, mahogany, oval shaped mirror, my ordinary reflection reappeared again, making me think that I was crazy.

I felt confined inside my office block of white and cream, locked inside a tiny space of four grey half walls, staring at a computer screen. While taking a bite of my sandwich, soggy and unappealing, I daydreamed of the wolf creature looking back at me, as though it were my own reflection. Black mirrors of technology didn't seem to make the beast appear, and I longed for that comfort, away from being trapped in life. It was a possibility that all of this wasn't real, my imagination trying to help me escape the life of screaming taunting, the voices deep inside my mind, pressuring me to do better, that I was better off dead; all the things the wolf stopped my brain from thinking. My chest felt tight, closing in on itself, as the murmurs inside chattered away, pushing me into a corner, whispering into my ear telling me I wasn't any good.

I rushed to the bathroom in a panic, dizzy and out of control. I pushed the heavy, metal doors open, falling into the room, where everywhere was quieter. No one around, just as I liked it. The overhead lights flickered, and the cubicles were tightly shut. The tiled, white floor, glistened from the reflections of the row of mirrors in front of me, above porcelain sinks with taps dripping water. The drip, drip, drip of the bedraggled water droplets, made me focus on my breathing. My ears opening to this rhythmic melody. I grabbed hold of one of the middle sinks, tightly with both hands either side, breathing shallowly, staring right into the depth of the basin and the darkness of the plug hole. As my eyes focused, water began travelling upwards up the pipes and filling up the space. The more I concentrated the more I soon realised, this was not water, but blood.

I jumped away in horror, watching the sink fill with red liquid, however when I moved backwards the blood disappeared, just like a sick and twisted magic trick. I moved closer, edging slowly with caution, my mind was once again playing cruel tricks on me. The mirror in front of me, showed me looking drained and tired, large bags had appeared under my eyes, because my mind was taking over my sleeping pattern. I would often lie for hours just staring up at the blank ceiling of my bedroom, watching shadows and lights from passing cars cast occasional light shows.

I blinked. Then I continued to blink, like a camera taking shots, until my long spindly eyelashes parted like curtains, showing me the wolf staring back at me again.

The creature was still, its eyes transfixed on my glare. The few bristles of fur swayed back and forth even though there was no breeze.

'How are you here? Can you travel from mirror to mirror? Is the world you appear to be inside connected?'

The wolf didn't move a muscle, just stood in the same position I was. When I rubbed my eyes, stuck with sleep, the wolf copied, her large, furry, grey paw and long sharp nails scratching its own eyes.

'Ow!' My own nails seemed suddenly as sharp and deadly, but looking at them with interest, I could see my fingers and fingernails still looked human.

I rubbed both eyes with my fists, this time carefully, staring at my reflection through my fingers. Just as before, the wolf rubbed its own black, curved, eyes with its paws. Large, knife claws scratching its own eyes out with no sign of any pain or screaming. I pulled my fists away from my face with force, seeing how the creature repeated the same movement.

Even though my hands were now by my side, I yelled in pain. The movement of daggers crawled through my eyeballs. A tiny drop of blood spilt from the corner of one eye and splashed in the basin.

I looked straight back at the mirror. With no emotion, the mute wolf's eyes started to bleed. The once river of onyx, was now pouring with the rush of deep scarlet, trickling down its fur. Its large mound of neck fur drenched in red, my own clothes reflected, covered in the stuff. I opened my mouth to scream but couldn't. The basin was now filling up with blood again, and as I tried opening and closing my eyes, telling myself this wasn't real, the pain in both my pupils stabbed me, like many injections being inserted all at once. My own plasma was pouring out of the corners of my optic nerves, I could feel my blood vessels popping inside my skull.

I couldn't move or speak, I just watched the blood flow into the sink in front of me, my clothes and skin covered in red. The pain was excruciating, as though half of my body parts were filling up like balloons. With as much effort as I could manage, I grabbed hold of the sink tightly, digging my nails into the porcelain, I looked at the reflection in the mirror.

Like me, the wolf was covered in blood, that stuck to her fur like glue, her eyes gushing, the only difference was this creature didn't seem to be in any pain whatsoever. I locked eyes with her, pleading for the pain to be over, screaming inside my mind.

'What do you want from me!'

There was silence from the beast, her blissful look turned into a smile, the corner of her mouth revealing large fangs either side. The wolf suddenly took one large bite and bit through her own arm, the skin through her fur bleeding out, all over the tiled floor.

It seemed that the creature and me had switched sides now. She was the commander, the one to decide what I was going to do next, and as I realised this, my left arm started to throb, as I looked my skin had shattered, my bones completely exposed and again blood gushed out, leaving puddles on the floor. I pressed my right palm on the wound, but the blood still ran. There was nothing I could do and it was all my fault.

'I feel faint ...' I thought. I fell onto the cold tiled floor, painted with my own blood, banging my head, and feeling my mind crack into a thousand pieces.

I was left lying there, unable to move, while I bled out from my arm and eyes, the floor around me filling up like a bath. From this angle, I could see part of the mirror hanging from the tiled wall. Mist and steam formed around the frame, until bloody paws peeked out, then each of its legs clambering from its captive mirror.

The wolf, drenched in blood, stood over me with no concern. Her breath smelt dead and rotting. I tried to speak back but the wolf just smiled, crushing my body with its boots, the boots I was currently wearing. It wandered off and pulled the large metal door to outside, leaving me helpless and dying on the cold floor, while blood surrounded me.

My vision was clouded with scratch marks, lights and hues bounced around my iris. My body felt too weak to lift, but I managed to raise my head from the bloody floor; it was then I first noticed the difference in my appearance. There was no tangled hair that rested upon my neck, but ashy grey fur that covered my entire face. My ears were no longer on the sides of my head but high and pointed. I blinked rapidly. In front me, my human body had been replaced by matted fur; a tail tucked in between my hairy, muscular legs. Everything I was witnessing was happening at a hundred miles per hour, and my sense of hearing heightened.

I could hear every droplet that fell from my skin, like it was flowing inside my brain. The door swung open, banging into the wall in urgency, the vibrations drummed and nestled into my mind, every little pin-drop felt like an earthquake.

A crowd began to gather around me, my head was unable to support itself anymore. I crashed to the ground, pounding my head once again, against the broken tiles. The conversations bled into my skull, my ears bleeding with the pressure. The last image I saw, a version of myself, hovering over my body, the twinkling eyes from the wolf in the mirror, staring into my soul, its teeth catching the light from the flickering lightbulbs overhead. This reflected my soul, laughing at me in the darkness.

Christmas Dinner

Sue Gerrard

I stamped my feet in impatience and to make sure they hadn't frozen and fallen off. The cold wisps of breath coming from my mouth seemed to wrap themselves around me like a cold shroud and they made me shiver even more.

Here I was at St Helens Junction Station on Christmas Day, waiting for a train I had not thought would be running and now doubted was going to come. I was beginning to think I was the victim of a joke. I was after all the only passenger here. A tear born of bone freezing cold trickled down my face.

I looked around and noticed a plaque which I read out of boredom more than interest. So, this station opened in 1830 and was one of the world's oldest. I found myself warming to this Victorian façade and wondered how many people had waited or arrived on this platform. I could see them milling around me, all with one thought in their minds, to arrive at their destination safely.

I read on, '... part of the Liverpool to Manchester line, the world's first passenger railway, originally called the "Bottom of Sutton Incline."' Involuntarily I stamped my feet again.

'I wouldn't keep doing that, it won't make the train come any faster.'

I turned around to see who the owner of the gravel voice was, an old railway guard; white haired and bearded with a ruddy face, probably due to standing on this freezing platform to nowhere because the trains seemed to have forgotten where the railway station was.

I was about to give a retort as sharp as the wind whistling around my head, but something in his demeanour stopped me dead. He had the air of someone who had been there forever, always waiting, never boarding, just waiting.

'You shouldn't be so impatient, in such a hurry to leave ...' he continued.

'It's arctic out here and no warmer in the waiting room.'

'You should be grateful there's a train service to Liverpool on Christmas Day ...'

He continued not acknowledging what I said.

'Yes, I suppose so.'

'Where are you going in such a hurry?'

'To my parents for Christmas Dinner, well it will be supper now.'

'Nothing wrong with that,' he said looking down towards the gaping tunnel, 'it will be here soon, mark my words.'

'I was going to spend it with my fiancé but ...' Why was I telling him all this?

'Fiancée, pretty, young thing like you shouldn't be tying herself down at, what are you? Twenty-one, twenty-two. There's a whole world out there, not like in my day.' he sniffled.

'Twenty-four.' And even though it could be said at today's level of political correctness he was bordering on sexual harassment, I didn't take offence. In fact, I felt rather comforted, it was as if he had seen it all before and it would all work out well in the end.

'I was going to drive.'

'These roads will put us out of business; I've worked here man and boy that I have.'

'I think your job is safe. The roads are blocked, just look at today, I was going to drive but there's been a bad accident on the M62 motorway, impossible to drive, that's why I'm here.'

'They reckon this station will close soon ...' I was sure I saw tears in his eyes. I was trying to work out how old he was; he looked in his eighties but couldn't be, it was just the whiteness of his hair, red complexion and the way he stooped made me think he was so old.

'What will you do if the station closes?' I asked.

'Dunno, spend more time with the misses I guess, although I don't think she'll take kindly to that, she hates me meddling in household things, that she does. See it's like now she's in a huff because I'm working Christmas Day, she doesn't see I'm on triple time for doing it. No, she just thinks I just want to mess up her Christmas dinner, that she does.'

'So when will you eat?'

'When your train's gone, then I'll hurry home just in time for burnt goose. The old gal can't cook but I daren't tell her that, oh no.'

I laughed. 'Sounds like my mum.'

He laughed, then said: 'See here's some more passengers coming across Pudding Bag Bridge to keep you company—won't be long now miss.'

I turned to see a middle-aged couple and a young girl, about 8, stepping onto the platform. They nodded.

'Won't be long now.' he repeated for their benefit, touching his cap.

'I am so glad there is a train, that accident on the M62. Two cars collided; I believe.' The man said in a grumpy voice, 'how can two cars going the same way collide?'

'Billy, think of the injured. I know this is inconvenient, but it could have been worse.'

'I guess so Eileen, it's just that I wanted to get Sacha,' he nodded towards the child, 'to our son's in time for Christmas dinner.'

'The world won't end because we'll be a little bit late.' His long-suffering wife said.

'We are going to be a lot late.'

The guard said: 'I was just telling miss here.'

'Leonie.'

'Leonie, strange name, my Martha, my misses will be really annoyed with me for being late ...'

'What do you have to do?' Billy asked more out of politeness than interest, 'I am sure we can get on the train when it comes if you want to get off.'

'Oh no sir, couldn't do that, it's my duty to see you board the train and then change the signal to red at the junction, so you won't run full into another train coming the other way.'

'On Christmas Day?' Eileen asked.

'This is a two-way service ma'am, yes, it is.' he said bowing his head.

Then it came quietly, like a slow heartbeat rising to a crescendo of power, then silence as it stopped at the platform.

The front carriages seemed to be full so encouraged by the guard we went into the last carriage grateful for the warmth.

'Goodbye miss.' the guard said, patting my shoulder and before I could respond he had disappeared, presumably to hurry home for his burnt goose.

***

The guard looked at the cobwebs on the Waiting Room window and a grimace of pain crossed his face. It never got any easier, no matter how many times he waved off the train.

The signal would stay green as it had all those years ago when he had forgotten to change it. Forgotten because he had been hurrying home for his burnt goose, hurrying up to please Martha.

The train would crash again and again ... but with new dead, still warm dead on it.

It was his job to see them safely on board. It was his penance, his shame, a shame over the deaths of two hundred and thirteen people that led to his suicide and now he was paying the perpetual price.

There would be more passengers tomorrow, another road crash, another victim to start their onward journey.

Twelve Shells

James Hancock

Ride hard, Death's dark mare, and collect those of poisoned heart. Fuelled by rage, the beast of pain and suffering carries souls to the gates of hell. And the name of the beast is Vengeance.

***

You can't be in two places at the same time. I was out on a trap collect on the night they came. The night my life turned inside out. I should have been home. Home, a funny word for a rundown shell of what once was.

Where to start? Let's go back to the beginning. Not the very beginning, but the beginning of the end, if you will. Population booming and pollution destroying vegetation meant one thing ... a lack of food. A serious lack, which moved from starvation to conflict. It got so bad that the so-called peacekeepers of the planet were bombing the shit out of their neighbours for extra soil in which to plant their crops. What does a bombed country do? They fight back, and use whatever they've got. Biological weapons. The last thing a dying world needed. Needless to say, things went from bad to catastrophic to apocalyptic in less than ten years.

Fourteen billion earthlings reduced to ten million. That's less than one survivor in every thousand. What was left was a world of disease and toxicity.

Over time, people came together and pooled resources, knowledge, and plans for a better future. But some didn't. Some came together with the like-minded approach of take what you can and fuck anyone who tries to stop you. Crazies and scav dogs hunted in packs; hunted the new-worlders. People like me. I was a third gen; those that knew little of the world before. The first gen were the survivors. The second gen were their offspring; rich with tales of 'life before'. The third gen were those that knew little of the old ways, and whose life expectancy wasn't great. Not that anyone's was. If the diseased earth didn't starve you, and the toxic water didn't poison you, the scav dogs and crazies would end you.

Scav dogs: scavengers. Hunters of anything and everything. Crazies: cannibals. Psychos that would happily reduce their number rather than starve. Both were bad. Real bad!

Mother Nature had a way of playing the crap hand the humans had dealt her, and she provided as best she could ... for the animals. Rabbits became as common a meal to a third gen as a loaf of bread to an old-worlder. Out of the weed-covered buildings and burnt out roads, into the urban wild of gardens, back streets, and abandoned industrial estates; that was rabbit country, and that's where trappers like me would gather our resources. That's where I was when the crazies came knocking.

Home, once a shopping mall, and now a broken shell of what it was. Memories of laughter, family, prosperity, greed, all wiped away. All that remained were the brick walls and smashed out glass windows. Wife, daughter, maker, stitcher, finder, reader, and cook; seven of our eight were at home in the old mall when the enemy crept in and changed my life.

I returned to scraps. The red aftermath of a frenzied food party. Just enough left to tell the story, but not enough to bury. Some bones taken for broth, or to be fixed and fashioned into something. Was my daughter's skull now the head of a crudely made club? Did her beautiful green eyes bob atop a bubbling pot? Horror of all horrors.

Through tears, I growled and ground my teeth in an uncontrollable rage. I only had one thing left now, one thing to live for. Revenge!

I prepared for death. Hatchet through belt loop, hard jacket fastened to the neck, and gun in hand; a shotgun, sawn and rusted, only to be used if really needed due to the limited supply of cartridges, and the unlikelihood of ever finding more. Twelve shells. If there was a god, I had only one prayer ... let me live long enough to fire them all.

***

Trappers know tracks and I followed the crazies with ease, all the way back to the outskirts of town. A rundown school, covered with graffiti and abuse. Smashed windows, collapsed walls, and large sections of roof missing and replaced with sheets of corrugated iron. The ruin of what once was. Fire pits glowed and flickered in the half-light of dusk. Voices boomed, cackling laughter, and a scream. A woman's scream. It was the scream of someone I knew. My stitcher, Cassie. If I hadn't let my anger override my grief, I would have made the puzzles into six people and known that one was missing.

Cassie had been moved here as fresh meat.

She screamed again. My mind ran wild with what they'd be doing with long knives and big hooks. No time to scout and plan. No time for anything anymore.

I crouched low, and using it as cover, passed the stripped carcass of a long-forgotten car, past what remained of a broken school gate, and hurried into the hornet's nest through a hole in the wall where the main reception doors once lived. The lobby area. Once upon a time, children would line up here and have their heads patted as a teacher counted them into assembly in the adjoining hall. Now it was the common room for ten cannibals.

The crazy in the entranceway was wearing a coat of skin, threaded with long pieces of bone to make armour. Waste not, want not. Crazies find a use for most things.

By the time he'd seen me, it was too late. He'd failed his watch! My hatchet came down hard on his forehead and split it like a ripe melon. Crack! He didn't have time to cry out and alert anyone, but the noise of his skull splitting had alerted them anyway.

The nearest crazy was sitting on an age-old chair; once a red-cushioned masterpiece of craftsmanship, now a faded, torn and urine-soaked arse rest, as some called a proper seat. The crazy's eyes widened, and he was about to shout a warning, but there was no need; both barrels from my gun went off and his face redecorated the wall of the school's library corner.

I stepped in, loading as I did, and looked around for my next target ... two big men dropping an old cooking pot and pulling shanks from belts.

No sooner had I clicked the gun shut, I'd brought it up and pulled the trigger. The first crazy flew backwards as his chest exploded. The second turned with the impact of shot thumping into his shoulder. He cried out and steadied himself for the advance, raising a crude knife with his good arm. My hatchet was on him before he could decide whether to charge or retreat. His knife hand was removed, and he squealed like a pig. My second strike was into his face, swiftly ending his screams.

The school hall erupted with life as the remaining six crazies jumped up from their idleness, left Cassie hanging on a length of hook and chain, and reached for the closest weapons to hand.

I reloaded and fired off two shells. One missed peppering hall wall, but the other found its mark in a crazy's neck. He collapsed, gurgling and struggling to breathe as he clutched his throat, attempting to win the battle for survival. He would lose. It would take a good long and agonising minute, but he would lose.

I ran past the hall entrance and down a corridor lined with classrooms. The crazies shrieked and roared as they made chase. Half my shells gone, half the crazies down, I turned and fired at the fastest of my enemies as he closed behind me. Thrown into a wall, he dropped and bent double, no longer a threat. His struggle would be long and forgotten, bleeding out from a mortal wound to his lower abdomen.

My second shot spat, flared, and hissed to nothing. A dud! My gun had failed me, and the closest crazy threw himself onto me like a possessed animal, dragging me to the ground and snapping out with sharpened teeth. You can't bite your way out of a hatchet fight. My weapon found its mark and split his head wide. So deep was the blow that *my* hatchet became *his* hatchet. No returns. I gave up trying to pull it free and rolled through a doorway and into a classroom before the next savage could join the melee.

I kicked out and shut the classroom door with my foot. A door ... such an underrated thing. A lifesaving thing. If there was a god, I owed it thanks for that small gift.

I didn't have time to block the door, or get some weight in the way to hold it shut, but I did have time to click open my shotgun, let the shells fly free, and push two new ones into place. Boom! Both barrels at once into the crazies as they broke through and into the classroom. The first shrieked, fell, and rolled around in agony. He'd brought up his arms to protect his face, and his ulna, radius and forearm muscles were shredded.

The second crazy was forced back into the last. The last ... a huge beast of a man, so hairy and fierce he was more bear than human. He threw the dead crazy out of the way as I loaded in my last two shells, snapped the barrel shut, and had my hand stamped on with force and precision.

The bear crazy roared with rage. Broken fingers, I cried out in pain. The bear crazy landed on me and brought down an axe, meant for my head, but meeting floor instead. I turned, wriggled, and tried to roll, but the force of my opponent was too much. I grabbed my shotgun with my good hand and brought it round to fire as the bear crazy smashed his axe into my clavicle. The pain was a blast of intense white heat. My shoulder was split to the bone. Boom! Thank God the shell was good. The barrel of my gun had touched the chin of the berserking bear when it went off, and I was blinded by the spray as his face burst and scattered.

His weight winded me, and my injuries made removing him a task, but I broke free, staggered to my feet and held my bloody and broken shoulder.

A downed crazy is not an out crazy, and the torn forearms of my previous enemy had hampered but not fully retired him. One shell left. Too good for him. I applied the boot and ended him like the dog he was.

On to Cassie with haste and see what good she could do for my wounds.

My 'luck' had finally run out. Cassie hung lifeless on her rusty hook. Holes where holes shouldn't be, she'd bled out into half a dozen buckets placed under her.

Sorry, Cassie, this wasn't a rescue mission. This was goodbye to the darkest and most brutal of worlds. A cruel and unforgiving world of horror.

There was only one thing left for it. I sucked barrel and squeezed trigger. It flared and flamed, but didn't finish. Another dud. My lips and cheeks were split to a crisp, and several teeth were shattered, but I lived. Why? Why had number twelve not concluded matters? The pain was excruciating, but I held on to consciousness. Barely.

I spat blood and teeth, stepped close to Cassie as she hung before me, and I thought ... I thought for the first time during this frenzied episode of madness. Was there a god? Did it have plans for me? Why was I still alive?

I pulled Cassie's needle kit from her pocket, staggered, and sat in the arse rest.

I would fix up and restart. It would take time, but I'd find a new path; a path that forgot the life of a husband and father. I would embrace the darkness that had enveloped me. Sick of rabbit, I looked at Cassie and the crazies; there was enough meat here to last a month.

If there is a god, I'll show it crazy. An unusable arm and a torn face, but a gifted extra life. I'd done good and respectful; now it was time for savagery. Depending on the god that kept me, I would either delight or disgust them. There would be no half measure. Rage and hate would be my fuel. I would become a relentless hunter of men. I would become death.

The Ghost of Home

Elizabeth Catherine

The emptiness echoed through the house, the walls and furniture a dull version of their former selves. A stark contrast to the bright blue sky outside, the birds singing under the sun.

She looked over her desk and out of the window and thought back to the day the colour left. It was a day that started out surprisingly well, considering how it ended.

It was a slow, quiet morning. The signs were there, an unusual silence hung around the unkempt house. Cups sat around unwashed and half full, like it had been left in a hurry. At first it gave this air of there being an emergency and nothing else mattered. What was left now was a haunting feeling, the ghost of that day comfortably living there. Taking up more space than even the living occupants.

She was pulled back to the present by voices passing by. An indistinguishable whisper travelling on the soft summer breeze. It almost sounded like a laugh.

It's all in your head, she told herself. That had become a daily habit, every time she passed a mirror showing her a face she no longer recognised. Though everything had started to feel unfamiliar, friends, family and home. Shells of their former selves.

Love didn't exist. Not anymore.

She forced herself up and jumped at the creak of the chair. The first loud sound for what felt like days. She collected all the stray cups and plates and took them to the kitchen. There was a noticeable layer of dust covering every surface, she paused and ran a finger along the counter. It was like a mix of dust and ash, an impossible amount for the short time it had been. Was it really there? That question in all its variations had been asked a lot recently. Did that really happen? Is that really what was said? Why am I so hurt?

Out the window, the day was still perfect, it was like it was taunting her.

Ivy making shadows of leaves along the kitchen floor. The cups and plates remained unwashed on the side. A reflection in the window caught her eye, it was her and she looked gaunt, too thin. She put her hand to her cheek, and it didn't feel that hollow. Her eyes were clouded, angry and sad. She looked so tired. Maybe it had been longer, maybe time was moving differently for her now. Too slow and too fast all at once, the endless years already waiting for peace and to feel the love that felt empty and more like a show than real love. Too slow, the days with nothing really to do. Time that was what was needed, that was what she told herself over and over. And now here she was lost confused and trapped in a house filled with spectres of the past, happy memories, tinged with this question mark of was any of it really real? Or was she so good at lying, she had convinced herself they were real?

The horror and fear left her body and was quickly replaced with regret and the feeling that now she was truly alone. Caught in a colourful web of confusing memories and images, moments in time that she would never get back. People she may never get back or talk to again.

A breeze making the leaves on the ivy rustle, and it sounded like whispers and laugher. She wonders if she should try to reach out, find anyone willing to help. Be there and help her untie these knots she had tied around herself. Make this panic feel not like an overwhelming wave ready to drown her. She melted to the floor away from her reflection, leaving the outside world outside. She outlined the shadows of the leaves, more appearing for every leaf she drew on the floor. She was going mad, she tried to picture her friends' faces and they were faded, blurry around the edges or worse, they were horrifying. Visions of hatred all pointed at her, it always felt like they would be better off without her. The last few years had convinced her, she was never enough. She picked up her phone and tried to form a message. Her cry for help, and she was met by this blank page, with a long, lingering, blinking line and an empty space, begging to be filled.

Tell the truth. Let them in. They will help. That voice was too quiet a whisper among the screams that filled her mind. Trying, she still couldn't get a solid hold on those whispers. She felt like she was being torn apart.

Was she dead? Maybe. If she was, this was a shitty afterlife, but something that she probably deserved. Or did she?

She looked at where the leaves once were, and the ones that appeared were gone.

I must have pissed off a witch, she thought to herself. This had all the markings of a hex.

She took a deep breath and looked at the blue sky, it can't be all that bad if the sky could still be clear and blue in whatever hell she had found herself in.

A voice simply said 'air,' it bounced around in her head and she found it in herself to go outside and see if the sun could help. Shine some light into the darkness that had trapped her.

She felt like a rusted machine as she pushed herself up off the floor, she expected a creak that never came. She slowly, with determination, made her way to the door and stepped out onto the warm porch. Instead of the street of houses, a huge ravine stood before her and on the other side stood a figure. Too far away to make out any details. That stranger stood there continually waiting, never getting impatient or leaving. She wondered if it was one of her friends, or simply another lonely soul in this strange place. Or something worse altogether.

Hog Fever

Phill Campbell

I woke up with a start. A hog-squeal was ringing in my ears. Then I remembered there were no hogs on the farm any more. Pa killed them all when the hog fever broke out.

The bedside clock said half-past twelve. I opened the window and leaned out. A dry grass smell crept in from the dead cornfield out back, and across the yard a red light burned in the window of the old barn. I heard it again—a grunting squeal like the old boar used to make. The sound and the red light got inside my head and made me feel so hot and strange that I couldn't get back to sleep.

***

'What were you doing up in the middle of the night, Leah? I heard you walking up and down on the floorboards.'

'I couldn't sleep, Pa. I was so hot and restless, and I heard noises in the old hog-barn.'

Pa's face went tight and hard when he was angry. 'I told you to stop thinking about that place, Leah. Hogs are unclean creatures. We never should have had them on this farm. The Good Book says that Jesus drove the souls of devils into a herd of swine.'

'But Pa, I thought ...'

'That's enough, girl. Get on with your work and you won't have time for godless thoughts.'

The air outside was bone dry. I could feel it clawing the back of my throat. The yard was full of lumber and rusty machinery that Pa had never got round to fixing. A few scrawny chickens scratched around in the dust.

'I hope they're laying well today, Leah. I need a dozen eggs for the shop. Phew! I swear that walk from town gets longer every time.'

Martha's face was round and red and shiny. She held a basket in one hand and a brown paper parcel in the other. She put them both down and looked around the place like it was an old tramp she was itching to smarten up.

'This place has gone to seed since your Ma died but it could be turned into a real little gold mine. Your Pa just needs the right kind of help to manage it.'

'Pa don't need nobody but me,' I said sulkily.

She gave me a bright smile. 'You've been his ministering angel, Leah, everyone knows that. But you're 16 now. You'll be wanting a man and a home of your own soon, and what'll your Pa do then? He'll be all alone on this place.' She held out the parcel to me. 'Here, I brought you a present.' I stared at her. My birthday was three days ago but no one had remembered it. 'Go on, open it.'

I pulled the package open and a green waterfall poured through my fingers. I'd never seen a dress so fine and silky before. The fabric clung to my rough skin.

'You'll sure catch the boys' eyes wearing that,' she laughed. 'Go on, scoot. But don't let your Pa catch you wearing it.'

Pa wouldn't let me have a mirror in my room so I used the reflection in the window pane instead. I looked like a different person wearing the dress. The fabric slid across my skin like cool water from the creek, and I felt something change inside me. Then the room went dark. I'd forgotten to close the door.

'You take that thing off right now,' Pa said.

I stood there in my shame and watched Pa's fingers knot and twist and tear the flimsy dress into rags. I couldn't look at his face.

'I warned you, Leah. I knew what you were after I caught you in the hog-barn that time. You're a little whore, just like your Ma was.'

***

The hog sounds woke me in the night and when I opened my eyes the red light was inside my head. The noises were everywhere, squealing and grunting, like an invisible herd was milling around me. But all I could see were the rags of the green dress lying on the floor in the moonlight. I lay there tossing and turning, thinking I was going mad. The hog-voices whispered things inside my head, vile, unspeakable things about Ma and Pa and Martha, and I couldn't make them stop. I could only lie there and listen to them.

***

'What are you doing here, Eddie?' He hadn't seen me follow him into the barn and he jumped when I spoke to him.

'Jesus, Leah, what'd you sneak up on me like that for? I thought it was your Pa coming up behind me.'

'Pa's gone to a chapel meeting. There's no one else here. It's been a long time since we played here when we was kids, Eddie. What'd you come back for?'

He was bigger than I remembered and his arms were muscled from working in his Pa's garage. A patch of dark hair showed where his shirt was open at the neck.

'It's sure changed a lot in here since we was kids. The place is falling to bits now.'

I looked around and saw that he was right. An elder bush grew through a hole in the wall next to an old trough powdered with hog meal. A pile of dirty straw lay in a corner with a cracked lantern hanging above it, and a rusty pitchfork leant against the wall. The place smelled of dust and weeds, and the ghosts of the hogs that had once lived there.

The hog-smell got inside my head and into the place where the red light burned and where I wore a green dress. The hog-voices told me what to do, and the wrongness of it melted my belly like warm sweet molasses.

Eddie pushed me away roughly and I stumbled against the wall. 'What the hell are you playing at, touching me like that?'

'Didn't you like it?'

'Look, Leah, I'm seeing someone. All right?'

'Who?'

'Never you mind who. But her Ma and Pa don't know about us, and this is a good place for us to meet. That's the reason I come here today, not to see you.'

The world turned red around me and the hog-voices pounded in my ears. I sank to my knees and when I looked up, Eddie was gone.

***

That night I sat on the edge of my bed staring at the heap of green rags on the floor. Pa had come back from his meeting and gone to bed early without looking at me. I felt all alone in the house. At midnight I went to the window and looked out. The red light was burning in the barn and I heard a low grunting noise, with now and then a sharp hog-squeal rising through it. The sound grew louder as I walked across the yard with the red light burning at the back of my eyes. I pushed the barn door open and went inside.

The red light was everywhere and the air smelled hot and raw. The grunts and squeals were deafening now. My heart thumped, and a sick sweetness filled my belly. Something was moving on the pile of straw in the corner. I saw a bristled hog-back gleam in the red light. Then its head came up, and it wasn't a hog's head, it was a man's; and a girl's arm snuck around his back from where she was lying underneath him. And I knew who they were and why they were meeting in the hog-barn, and I hated them both.

I remembered how Pa had slaughtered the herd after they caught hog fever. He said it was the only way to kill the evil in them. So I took the rusty pitchfork from the wall and stabbed down with it. It went in easier than I thought.

Martha screamed and rolled out from under Pa's body, pushing it over onto the floor. She screamed again when she saw his blood all over the nice print dress she'd bought at the Home and County Store. But I was staring at Pa's face, remembering his hands tearing the green dress ... remembering how his hands had torn at my dress once before, when we was alone together in the hog-barn.

Martha was gone now and she wouldn't come back. There was only me and Pa left now. Like I told her, Pa don't need nobody but me.

The Cormorant

Mark Konik

'There's no Wi-Fi,' Tamara called to her mum.

'Why don't you explore the beach?'

Tamara had wanted to stay with her dad. He lived across the road from the ocean baths, where she hung with her friends. Instead she was here. Her mum had booked a week in a beach house in a remote part of the coast just north of Forster. The house was small but neat. It had two antique fishing rods hanging on the wall and some old newspaper articles that had been put into frames.

Picking herself off the lounge, Tamara set off for the beach. As she left the house a southerly blew into her face which made her pull up the zipper on her sweater. After looking up and down the shoreline, Tamara headed to the rock pools that were at the near end of the beach. She noticed a girl, about her age, bending down looking into one of the pools. Tamara thought that a friend might make her holiday less tiresome and walked towards her.

When she got to the girl, Tamara saw that the girl was only wearing a pair of boardshorts and t-shirt. She must have been freezing.

'Hi,' called out Tamara. The girl turned around and smiled. Tamara noticed that the girl had pigtails, and one of her front teeth was chipped.

'Aren't you cold?' asked Tamara.

'Wanna see something cool in the big rock pool over there?' The girl gestured with her head towards a larger, deeper rock pool not far from where the waves were crashing.

Tamara was unsure if to follow the girl as she waved her hand for Tamara to follow her. She decided to go and was careful not to fall and cut herself on the jagged rocks. The waves continued to thump down and make the rocks slippery. They arrived at the big rock pool just as a wave filled it with water. Once the foamy top had disappeared, Tamara noticed why the girl was so excited. There was a long silver fish caught in the rock pool darting around looking for an escape.

Before the next wave came to fill the rock pool, the girl jumped into the rock pool, the water reaching above her waist. She put her hands into the water, and grabbed the fish with one fell swoop and brought it to the surface. Its scales were grey with a sliver of purple that were illuminated in the afternoon sun.

'What a catch! How'd you do that?' called Tamara. The fish was thrashing side to side, the girl holding it like a trophy.

'Are you gonna take it home and eat it?' asked Tamara.

'Do you want to?' replied the girl.

Tamara shook her head, 'No.'

The girl smiled, 'Me neither.' She placed the fish back into the water and it sped under a rocky ledge. The girl climbed out of the rock pool and stood next to Tamara. Even though the wind had picked up and the girl had been in the cold water, she wasn't shivering. The two of them left the rock pool and walked back towards the shore.

Just beyond the breakers, Tamara could see some birds diving into the water. The birds were circling a school of baitfish. The girl saw Tamara watching the birds plunge into the blue and answered Tamara's question before she could ask it.

'It's a cormorant. They nest up in the cliffs,' and pointed above where they stood. 'They're such beautiful birds.'

The girls could hear someone calling in the distance and turned to see Tamara's mum waving.

'I think you might have to go,' said the girl.

'I'll be back,' said Tamara. 'Did you want to come and have a look at our beach house?'

'Maybe next time.' The girl gave her a smile. Tamara left her new friend and ran to her mum.

'Where were you? I was worried,' asked Tamara's mum.

'You're the one who told me to go exploring.' They started walking back towards the house.

Once at the house, her mum pointed to a plate on the table. 'I've made you some jam sandwiches.' It wasn't until then that Tamara realised how hungry she was.

'How was the beach?'

'Great, I met a girl that showed me a huge fish that was caught in one of the rock pools.'

Her mum winked at her, 'Told you we didn't need Wi-Fi.'

As Tamara ate her second jam sandwich, she started to look at the newspaper articles that were hung on the wall. There was one about a man that had won a medal at a lifesaving competition at Bondi Beach. The other, which hung near the kitchen window, was about a small girl that had drowned down at the beach. Tamara read the date and it was from before she was born. She looked at the picture of the girl that had drowned and stopped chewing her sandwich. The girl in the picture had pigtails, and one of her front teeth was chipped.

Tamara looked at the picture again. She put her plate on the sink and called out to her mum, 'I'm going back down to the beach.'

Tamara ran back to the beach. The late afternoon sun had turned the water a hazy grey. As she got there, she saw that the incoming tide had swallowed the rock pools. She looked for the girl, but could see nothing.

Just as Tamara was turning to go back, a cormorant with its wings spread wide, swooped over her shoulder and let out an elegant call. Tamara stopped to look at it. The cormorant glided over the top of the breaking waves and dove into the water. In one fell swoop it dived down, brought a fish to the surface and flew back to its nest in the cliffs.

Tamara smiled to herself and walked back to her mum who had followed her to the beach. They turned and walked along the shoreline. Tamara didn't even notice that the wind was blowing more fiercely than before.

Movement Detected

Frederick Pangbourne

Dale Foster was aroused from his dreamless sleep for reasons that eluded his half-conscious state. It was apparent, though, that something had interrupted his subliminal rest, pulling him back into the realm of cognisance. With his eyes still closed, he inhaled deeply, releasing his breath slowly as he shifted beneath the warmth of his covers; and attempted to find a comfortable position that would lull him back to sleep. It was then the elusive sound that had initially awakened him, repeated.

'Movement detected,' the robotic female voice stated.

Foster exhaled again heavily as he was now abandoning any chance of rest and began awakening. Rolling over onto his back, he pushed the covers down to his hips before engaging in a full body stretch. Arms and legs extending as he yawned.

'Movement detected,' the voice repeated from the darkness outside his bedroom.

It was this second statement from his home alarm system that made him realise just how urgent the message was, and he abruptly sat up on his elbows. The words were now sinking into his still clouded head. Someone was in the house. Flinging the covers off him, he swung his legs over the bed and sat up, listening to any sounds within the dark house. As his eye adjusted to the darkness, he gazed at the open doorway of his bedroom. He sat there unmoving, listening to the stillness, waiting for any sound that would indicate an intruder. After about thirty seconds, when nothing was heard, he sat up from his bed. With his vision now fairly adjusted to the lack of light, he slipped to his closet door and retrieved a wooden baseball bat resting in the corner. Gripping the bat, he slowly made his way to the doorway of his room. Reaching out with a free hand, he gently felt along the hallway wall until he found the light switch and turned on the hall light.

His bedroom was on the second floor of the old Victorian home and, from where he stood in the hall, he could look down over the railing to the open foyer below. The first floor and the bottom half of the staircase leading down were obscured in blackness. Again, he listened intently for any sound.

'Movement detected,' the unexpected voice announced from the security panel just behind him on the wall, giving him a startling jolt and causing him to nearly drop the bat.

'Fucker!' he hissed and whirled about, turning his attention to the panel. Set at chest level, the eight-inch screen was lit green and displayed the words 'MOVEMENT DETECTED: KITCHEN'. Hitting the acknowledge button, Foster turned around and faced the hall railing again.

'Who's down there?' He shouted as aggressively as he could at two-thirty in the morning. 'I've got a gun, so if you're smart, you'll haul ass outta here!' He lied.

After declaring his warning, he leaned over the railing and peered down into the darkness, listening for any movement. The house remained silent. After a few minutes, when still no sound was heard, he sighed, and wondered if perhaps the central air had moved a curtain or something insignificant, setting off the electric eye downstairs. Still in nothing but his boxer shorts, he moved to the staircase where a pair of light switches were set on the wall. He hit one switch and the foyer below him was instantly illuminated. With the light now on, it gave him a small sense of courage and, with the bat still in his hand, he descended the stairs. The carpeted steps creaked slightly as he made his way down and Foster grimaced at the sound of his presence being announced.

In the foyer, he waited and scanned into the darkness of the living room to his left and the dining room on his right. Still, no sound was heard. Besides these two large rooms and a downstairs bathroom, only the kitchen remained at the back of the house.

'Hello?' he asked, now feeling foolish as he suspected the house was void of any outside intruders, and leaned toward the notion of a swaying curtain in the air's current. Still, just to make himself feel even more secure, he turned on the lights in both rooms, finding them without visitors. He then proceeded to the kitchen.

The kitchen, as with the two previous rooms, was also empty. One thing did, however, catch his attention as being out of place. The cellar door was ajar. He paused at the unanticipated sight and gripped the bat in both hands. Creeping ever so slowly, he inched to the cellar's threshold and looked down. Like the foyer before he had come downstairs, the basement was a void of blackness past the first few steps leading downward. It seemed, however that the darkness was blacker than the foyer and other rooms. It almost seemed tangible and thick.

'Who's down there?' he shouted down the wood steps and, as with his previous inquiries, no answer was returned. 'Well, if there is someone down there, you might as well get comfortable because you're down there for the night.'

Still no voice replied from the dark. Foster frowned at his own frightfulness and again felt foolish. It was apparent that he had not closed the door properly and the air had pushed against it with just enough force to cause it to swing open. It did not take a Hercule Poirot to solve this mystery. Re-closing the door, he locked it at the handle and jiggled it forcefully to assure it was properly closed this time. As added insurance, he secured the chain lock on the door's upper portion.

Nodding with satisfaction, he turned off the kitchen light and walked back to the foyer, where he turned off the lights to both dining and living room. He was just about to mount the stairs back to his bedroom when a familiar voice called out from above him.

'Movement detected.'

He froze with one foot on the first step. From the kitchen came the faint creaking sound of the cellar door slowly opening. That's impossible. His mind screamed. He had taken every step to secure it. The light in the upstairs hall suddenly went out, leaving him in the foyer's lone light. He could feel the hairs on his neck become erect. A primal fear was holding him in place. The sound of bare feet could now be heard walking across the kitchen's hardwood floors. He peered into the darkness of the kitchen and witnessed a shape moving in the lightless room. He found his mouth beyond dry, his tongue sticking to his palate. A bead of sweat was running down his bare back.

'Death imminent,' the alarm now proclaimed and despite his petrified state, he threw a confused glance up at the alarm. The screen was now glowing red. 'Death imminent,' it repeated.

A presence was now next to him, and he turned his head. Less than a foot from his face was another, beyond any nightmare imaginable. Large lidless red eyes met his own with their maniacal glare. A wide mouth filled with rows of long canine teeth grinned insanely at him as it wrung its clawed hands in glee. The nightmare was snickering at him. Foster felt hot urine running down his legs as his lips quivered uncontrollably.

'Death imminent,' he heard again from the upstairs hall just before the nightmare feigned a leap into his face and spat out, 'Boo!'

It was then the last light in the house extinguished itself and Foster screamed.

Out of Ancient Wallachia

Jonah Jones

'There's been another of them murders, sir,' Mrs Hayward informed him as she served breakfast.

'Really?'

'Local lass from Jericho. Nasty. Just like the last couple of 'em. Nasty.'

She served up the poached eggs and crisp bacon, followed by the devilled kidneys. Arfon Caradog restrained himself from wolfing the lot. That morning his appetite was monstrous to the point of being near painful and the taste of that girl lingered, yet he was delicate in the way he consumed his food. A gentleman before all else.

The devilled kidneys soon replaced any taste remaining from the previous night and, as he consumed the rest of his breakfast, he cast his mind back to the girl. A prostitute, alone at that time of night, so close the meadow, standing on display under the street gas-light between the mill stream and the canal. She had smiled at him and led him by the arm into the shadows. Hadn't screamed, hardly struggled as he took her blood. As she approached the moment of death, she simply sighed as if some great longing had been assuaged. Perhaps she thought something else was going on, until it was too late. Perhaps she was searching for release.

Her easy acquiescence had unsettled him. That night he had been aware of a sense of dread. Dread was something to be visited upon his victims, yet here was a victim that had induced it in him. He turned his mind away from himself and wondered that her body had been found so quickly. He'd left her covered up between the bridges but away from the canal. It was of no consequence. The police seemed to be particularly incompetent in the city of Oxford. Spending their time looking after the wealthy, they weren't going to worry overmuch about a street-walker.

Having broken his fast, shaved and completed his ablutions, the professor finished dressing, setting his starched wing collar and cravat in place carefully, before adding Macassar oil to his hair and smoothing it down, then putting on his frock jacket, trousers and cloak. From the hat hooks on the stair, he took his short-crowned top-hat and made his way to the History Faculty, where he greeted his fellows in the anteroom.

'You've cut yourself, old chap,' Doctor Phillips told him.

'Damn! Have I?' Caradog replied. 'Where?'

'Above the top lip.'

Caradog touched himself above his lip and saw blood on his finger.

'Better spruce myself up. Don't want to scare the little innocents, now do we?'

'Don't know why you bother with all that shaving rigmarole,' the well-bearded doctor added as Caradog made his way to the lavatories.

The professor smiled as he imagined the good Doctor's reaction should he ever explain why he was the only clean-shaven man amongst his peers. He dabbed at the wound until it dried sufficiently, before proceeding to the lecture hall where row upon row of expectant faces greeted him.

Taking his notes from his briefcase, he strode up to the lectern and addressed them all.

'Good morning, Gentlemen. Today's topic—the transmigration of souls as understood by the medieval Christian mind.'

As was his routine, he poured a glass of water, took a few sips and then continued 'Of course we have a problem when discussing these matters. According to orthodoxy, Christians believe in one life, one soul, The soul arrives in a body then returns to its maker when the body dies. Transmigration of souls was only the Hindus, wasn't it?'

He scanned their young faces. By their dull expressions, he knew he would need to work harder at sparking their interest.

'Let us not forget that Christianity was introduced to people who believed something else. That might be anything from Pantheism, through Zoroastrianism and Buddhism, to some very murky religious beliefs indeed. In the early stages of conversion, many in the congregation had simply added The Christ to what they already believed to be true, transmigration of souls being a case in point.'

He turned to the blackboard and as he did so, something slipped out of kilter, as if someone else had taken his mind's place. Instead of writing GNOSTICS on the board, as he had intended, he wrote GRIMFRIARS. He shook his head in an attempt to throw the usurper out, failed, then turned back to the audience.

'We don't know their original name but Grimfriars was the name given to a particular sect by the Catholic Church in its early years. Certainly they were regarded as dangerous heretics and for once, the Catholics were unquestionably right on both counts. These sect members attempted to capture souls for their unspeakable rites. They started off as British semi-Christians holding territory in Wallachia after the retreat from Eastern Rome when their leader Magnus Maximus was defeated and killed. Wallachia has the same root as Wales—meaning Celtish—as described by those that weren't of that tribal inter-relationship. Their religion became corrupted to the point that a modern Christian would find it unrecognisable save for the fact that they held the blood of Christ to be sacred and believed that their own blood could become sacred if purified by spiritual and physical absorption of others' blood. Later they became the Bogomils, meaning Dear to God—followers of a gnostic branch of Christianity.'

One of the undergraduates raised his hand and asked the question 'Would you refer to them as vampires, Professor?'

Caradog was pleased that one of his pupils had the gumption to ask it, proving that at least one pair of ears had been listening.

'A moot point. How do you define such a thing? They weren't anything but human, so they were inclined to take blood, rather than were forced to do so for their own survival. I am of the opinion that if you combine two of the most frightening diseases of medieval times, syphilis and rabies, consider their symptoms and cures, you may arrive at lycanthropy and vampirism.

'Syphilis—madness, jagged teeth, sensitivity to bright light. Rabies—also madness, together with great strength, hydrophobia and both diseases transmitted by a bite. And the cure? Mercury, quicksilver,' He paused for effect and to see if any of the undergraduates could work it out. No evident light behind any eyes, so he continued, '*in aliis verbis*—a silver bullet.'

Allowing that to sink into the collective mind, he added his personal codicil.

'I don't believe in vampires or werewolves. Yet of course there are those who do and furthermore, there are those that believe themselves to be of those persuasions. There are some demented individuals who believe there is a spiritual component in the physicality of blood and perhaps they may derive greater spirit by indulging in these practices.'

The rest of the lecture was a monologue as usual. He spoke of cults and breakaway groups in religious practices, intimated that the Knights Templar may have drifted into such beliefs more to stimulate the undergraduates but was unable to detect any desire on his audience's part to indulge in further intellectual intercourse. He might simply be listening to his own echo returning from the wood panelled walls.

They trouped out at the due time and as he was cleaning the blackboard, he felt something of a presence. He turned to see a young man at the very back of the tiered benches. The young man was staring at him and looking appallingly sad.

'Can I help you, sir?' Caradog called out.

The young man shook his head. 'I wanted to be a minister,' he said as he turned and left by the door at the top of the steps.

Disconcerted, Caradog continued cleaning the blackboard, rubbing out GRIMFRIARS and passing the duster over it and over it again as if to remove any evidence of what he knew to be out there and what he suspected might have crept inside him.

Having finished his public work for the day, Caradog found himself strangely at a loss. He walked down to the Castle Mill-stream and followed it to the Thames. With the railway and the strengthened banks of the urban waterway, it was hard to imagine how it must have looked when the drovers of the Dark Ages would have known it. Yet their ghosts were apparent to him and he was pleased to watch them and meditate upon time passing. There they were, the drovers of olden times with their corgis snapping at the heels of the black cattle. Dressed in beaver hats and capes against the weather, singing and swearing in the language of Cymru as they followed on their high stepping Welsh cobs. Hiraeth flooded him as he watched his compatriots making their way to the markets in London where the rich folk lived. The only place he knew of in Britain that translated directly from Welsh to English. Rhyd-ychen—Ox-ford. This was the last place one could cross the Thames with a herd of cattle upstream from London, and as such was equally important to Celt and Saxon. Name upon name. So much history in such a small place. Even so it had been little more than a small market town when the Grimfriars first arrived. He wondered what possessed him to tell the undergraduates about the Grimfriars. He cast his mind back to that singular moment. Another consciousness had usurped his mind and motivation, together with his sense of time and place. It was happening again as he recalled his feelings.

The clop-clop of horses' hooves and creak of carriage wheels caused him to look around to discover that he was back in St. Giles without any memory of having walked there.

Making his way past the Martyrs' Memorial, he took out his pocket watch. It was already well past nine in the evening and the fern crozier-shaped gas-lamp over the cab shelter was being lit. No time for dinner in the college, he would have to hurry.

Quickening his step, he walked along Little Clarendon Street and into Jericho, his favourite hunting ground, then out towards Wolvercote and the priory at Godstow. Always prepared, he felt the curved finger knives in his pocket as he crossed the bridge into the meadow.

The mist trapped by the hills in which Oxford rested, was knee high and he left a rising trail as he walked through it. Caradog found an elderly man walking distractedly on Walton Well Road and dragged him down into the mist, slashed his throat with the finger-knives and amongst the rough grass and ragwort, the monster feasted on the wretched man's blood.

A train gathered speed as it crossed Port Meadow, the lights of its carriages part-obscured by the mist, now shoulder high. Hiss, thump, hiss, thump, then rattle and clack, fading away into the night as it headed north, the smoke from the funnel following its maker. Soon, the living silence of the night, took her place. A nightjar churring over towards Wytham. A tawny owl pair telling each other where they were. He finished lapping at the blood, stood strong and replete for a time to enjoy the renewal, then began walking towards Wolvercote, the sound of his feet on the tussocks of grass hissed in his ears as he felt the pulse of the new blood refreshing both body and soul, raising him up until it felt as if he was floating towards his masters on a cloud.

Through Wolvercote, past the Trout Inn with merry singing from its customers, across the twin bridges and into the field outside the ruined Abbey at Godstow. God's place? Hardly. Not as things now stood. This was more surely the place of the Devil and his predatory followers.

The cadaverous, pallid faced Usher carrying a tallow lantern, came to meet him and led him into the inner chamber, whilst enquiring as to whether his teaching work was proceeding well.

'Yes,' he assured him, 'they seemed to show some interest today. Perhaps I am improving as a lecturer.' He smiled briefly, received no response, so returned to a sombre expression as they followed the light of the stinking, spitting lantern.

'They'll find you out,' a young female voice whispered, causing him to turn his head but there was no one standing as close as the voice had seemed, nor was there any female as far as he could tell beneath those dark, hooded robes. Caradog stepped onto the dais set before the cloth covered altar, the gold-threaded cloth throwing the tallow light back from its surface and causing even the Usher's face to glow with unnatural life.

The Chalice-bearer stepped forward and the Blood-letter approached as Caradog removed his cravat and unfastened his collar, exposing the glass tube and tap, set in his neck.

The Blood-letter turned the tap and the Chalice-bearer collected the blood as it pumped into the Vessel of Life. Once it was full, the tap was turned off and wiped clean as the Bearer gave the cup to each of the Grim-friars in turn as they chanted the canticle of renewal from the Book of Ancient Encounters before taking their portion, each by each.

His perception set a distance from reality, Caradog watched and listened as phantoms swept around him and whispered dark stories in the whirling smoke and smell of burning corpse fat.

He was still shaking when he returned to his rooms and fell into a disturbed sleep.

The next day, during another substantial breakfast he perused his schedule, then settled into some light reading for the morning. Nothing too strenuous, he felt that he needed a little time to himself. Time to re-cover. Time itself could become another warder.

Halfway through a chapter, something caused him to look up from his reading of Macaulay's History of England to see the wraith of a girl in the room with him, her blue lips pouting, her eyes fixed upon his, her feet stamping on the wooden floor as she marched upon the spot.

There was a knock on his study door.

'Come in,' he called out and a timid undergraduate presented himself. Oh yes—it was time for a tutorial. What was this one's name? Began with F, didn't it?

'Mister Franks.'

'Yes, sir.'

'Please sit.' The boy did so.

'Now then, what were we talking about last time?' Caradog picked up Franks' essay on his desk. He had given it a Beta plus mark. 'Ah yes. Cultural misappropriation.'

Now he was adjusted to the familiar role, the tutor began to expand upon the theme.

'Yesterday, not far from the ford that gives the city its name, I was meditating upon the name Rhydychen—the Welsh name for Oxford and I fell to thinking about my own name. Caradog is one of the few truly Welsh surnames. All the common ones—Jones, Evans, Williams, and suchlike were imposed upon the Welsh by the English—a form of cultural suppression, if you will. Like hunting witches and murdering them in the name of Christianity while stealing their symbols and their festivals for Christian use.'

The undergraduate showed, or feigned, interest. 'Or the Romans cutting straight roads through the country, no matter what the terrain,' he suggested.

Caradog was set to musing. 'The Romans—what a culture they had. Destroy a civilisation and then rebuild its remnants in their own likeness. An Empire greater than any before it. Greater than most before our own.'

The brand scar on his breast caught slightly on his shirt as he stood up, as if to remind him that his time was not his own. He looked at the clock.

'Thank you, Mister Franks. It has been stimulating.'

'Thank you, sir,' the undergraduate replied as he stood to leave.

Caradog handed him his essay with a smile. 'Next time, let us discuss that very subject—Christian iconography and symbolism acquired from other sources.'

'Yes, sir,' the other replied before leaving.

Caradog waiting until he could hear the footsteps leave the staircase, then opened his shirt to examine the raised scar of his branding. The circled cross of pre-Christian times. The four points of the ever-turning year, codified, simplified, to become a statement of thinking men's control over the chaos. They had burned the Celtic Cross into him, striving to tame this creature from the darkness before it came to know itself. Never part of that civilised world, he was being led into their constructions, like a wild aurochs with a metal ring though its fleshy nose. It was in the sound of the word—not its spelling. Aurochs—Ox - Oxford. The crossing of the river. This mind that he once called his own was certainly being led by someone or something outside that which belonged to him. The reddening scar seemed to be stinging as if it were open and rubbed with salt. Were they calling him? Could they make his flesh work to their advantage in such a way?

He looked at the clock once more. What time had it been the last time he looked? He couldn't remember.

For no particular reason, save but to immerse himself in a peculiar tangle of history and perhaps to supress the sense of being a prisoner of those warders that lived outside the city boundary, Caradog went to visit the Pitt-Rivers Museum. Passing the magnificent sign that informed him he was entering an area set with man-traps, he was transported to a place of somewhat thrilling fear, crammed with strange and exotic artifacts from the history of other peoples, other places. Britain owned all this section of the World and had brought back its treasures at which the population might marvel.

Once again, he found himself casting his eyes and his mind over the exhibition of shrunken human heads. Gruesome and fascinating in equal measure. Did the perpetrators of such meticulous crafts believe that they were extracting the essence of their victims? Was it that the Grimfriars reached South America? Perhaps they went across with the Conquistadores or maybe they had no need to travel. He didn't know for certain whether they were human, some other creature or even not made of flesh of any kind. Were they a creation of the human condition—the parasite in us all, externalised?

A museum staff-member politely informed him that the museum would soon be closing and so he made his way to the exits, following a few other patrons into the evening air, noting that a middle-aged woman was making her way into the University Parks and so Caradog followed her at a discrete distance as the murderers' friend, the mist, began to creep up from the Cherwell. He surmised that she was one of the adventurous and determined women who had taken up the idea of a place where they might be educated—Lady Margaret Hall. He had a sneaking admiration for these women, although he would never have admitted such in public. Not the done thing. Women's place and all that.

'I gets jealous of women like her. I never got the chance to be schooled proper.'

That young girl's voice again, closer than reality. Not expecting to see anything, he turned and looked all around. Other than the woman he had been following, there was nothing but the parkland, the sky and the rising mist. Now he, the shadow stalker, began to experience menacing shadows inside his own mind. He turned back from his potential victim. He didn't need to feed that evening and neither did the Masters. What he did need was to understand what was happening to him or to distract himself from the issue.

After a light supper, he took up his copy of The Strand Magazine and read the latest Arthur Conan Doyle—a Sherlock Holmes story entitled *The Adventure of the Crooked Man*. Always so satisfying, Sherlock Holmes. Everything was elementary to him. The world made utter sense to the man. A person in charge of his own life and largely that of others affording that sought-for distraction from the cruel truth of the real world.

Deciding to retire early, he lit a candle and took it into the bedroom where he sensed immediately that he was not alone.

'Who are you?' he asked the empty room, moving the candle from side to side that he might better see in the shifting shadows.

'Little Jaqueline,' came the reply.

'Do I know you?'

'Yes.'

'Why cannot I see you?'

'My body is no longer here. You have taken me into yours.'

His hand holding the candlestick began to tremble and then to shake uncontrollably. He dropped the candlestick and the flame was extinguished. In the darkness he asked 'Why didn't you struggle?'

The creature inside his head proffered no reply but simply laughed long and loudly as he sank to his knees and bowed his head.

'Prayin' won't do you no good.'

'I know that,' he near-sobbed, for God wouldn't be listening to the likes of him and who was left to hear his prayer but the Devil himself?

***

The next morning, he asked Mrs Hayward how she knew about the girl being murdered before the newspapers had arrived at the lodge.

'Miss Charben, Professor Grange's housekeeper told me, Sir.'

'And did this young woman have a name?'

'Don't know, sir.' She thought about how to express it and then added 'She wasn't what you might call a good girl, sir.'

He nodded sagely in response, then cast his mind back to the encounter. One element dominated his memory. She seemed to be pleased to die. The more he concentrated upon her dying face, the more he believed she had been seeking release. Why, therefore was she haunting the very person who had provided that release?

Having a free day, he ambled through the town, along the Cornmarket and past Carfax to the newly opened municipal library in St Aldates where he perused the newspapers. There it was in the Oxford Times. A few paragraphs devoted to the story. They didn't go into detail about her lifestyle or personal history, nor yet her place of residence. He'd learned more from his housekeeper. One unexpected fact stood out for him. The murder victim was named Mary Pope. There was no mention of anyone named Jaqueline.

One day he saw her, the next he couldn't see her at all. One day she is silent, the next she is speaking to him with a certain convincing authority. Mary or Jaqueline, she was dead and he had taken her blood. What he was now experiencing was entirely inside his mind. It seemed to him that he needed to adopt a different perspective.

As they were trying to control him, so he was trying to control his own self. Some part of his self-control was slipping, failing to keep the wilder side under control. He was losing himself. In meditation he found himself wandering the woodlands of Bosnia, the place of his twisted spirit's birth. These dimly lit forests were home to the creatures of darkness; the werewolf and vampire, the hobgoblin, battle-hag and soul drinker. He had passed through many lives already before the Bogomils found him and part-tamed him. It had pleased him to live as a solitary wild creature yet had been tempted by the warmth and comfort of the citizens' homes. They fed him, he fed them—the balance was mutually beneficial. He recalled how simple it had been to be a semi-domesticated animal and smiled in his reverie.

Then the Grimfriars rose to power as the Bogomils were persecuted and scattered by the Catholics in their holy certitude. Like the Bogomils, they held flesh in low esteem and believed in the power of blood to invigorate and renew but unlike the Bogomils, the Grimfriars had no respect for those that served them. The relationship between soul drinker and his husbandmen changed. These monks demanded, they enchained, they hoodwinked and they kept him hungry as a nobleman's falcon.

They held him in a thrall beyond his understanding. Wherever they spread their influence, so he was born again to be with them. They had brought him from the mystical mountains of Preseli to this last crossing of the river for the cattle.

Another murder was due, another bloodletting, another visit to the Grimfriars.

On this occasion, they seemed deliberately distant, questioning. He was tempted to think that they were colder than usual and almost laughed at the thought. They were utterly without warmth in the first place. They were his masters and he was no more than a slave providing them with sustenance.

They turned the tap and the blood flowed into their cup as their provider became lightheaded and dreamed of being in another place, any other place. A place where he no longer had to face these creatures of the darkness. Once again, he found himself smiling. He was as much a creature of the darkness as they. He was the death bringer. They merely fed upon his victims.

He sensed that they didn't like him smiling in such a place dedicated to the dark, gloomy and faceless. Once they had taken their fill, one of them asked him what he found amusing.

It was as if he were a naughty schoolboy.

'I think I was falling asleep,' he told them.

'You are less vigorous than you once were.'

He wondered whether that was an observation, a criticism or a threat. Were they expecting more from him? He was providing all they needed—or so he had thought until that moment. Was his blood any thinner? Were they tasting the difference?

Questions assaulted his spinning head. His eyes were shuddering as if they refused to accept what they were seeing. There were voices inside his head and out, demanding more than he was able to give. An army arrayed its ranks against him, while he stood alone. Yet not so. These others inside his mind were not simply demanding, they were also trying to take control of his thoughts and actions.

In the midst of all this confusion, the line of Grimfriars had accused him of being less vigorous.

What would they know? They hadn't known what it was to be alive for centuries.

In the failing light, he made his faltering way back through the darkened village of Wolvercote, not trusting himself to walk through the meadow. He realised that he should stay on firm roads and move from town light to town light as much as he could. This was new depth of darkness, one that was encroaching upon his very soul, and he knew that he was in jeopardy.

She wanted him to know why she was inside his mind and so she focussed all her power. That night was the worst he had experienced to that juncture, although it seemed as if he was seeing the world through another's eyes. He found himself in a factory, working a weaving machine of some variety. At first confused, he quickly adopted the persona and knew that he was in the blanket mill in Witney. He felt the heat, the ache in his arms, was near deafened by the clacking of the machinery and knew that he was Mary.

A strong hand gripped her arm and began to lead her away towards the back of the factory where they kept the bales of wool. She was powerless against the strength of the man who threw her onto the scattered wool and proceeded to take her as if she were a ewe and he a ram. Other men joined in, violated her as cruelly and then left her curled up against the wall, sobbing as her blood seeped into the raw wool.

The man that was Arfon Caradog fought to the surface of this nightmarish flood of twisted memory in which he was drowning. He lit the candle and staggered over to the mirror to stare at his face, drawn in terror. It was still the man. He continued to examine his own reflection. He looked as if he'd run a hundred miles from some monster. But how could he run from the monster that was his own self?

The candle guttered and then burned out. He smelled the human fat of the Grimfriars' candles. He felt his own heart rate begin to rise and then he—no she—was running away from the workhouse dormitory to the city.

Time, unreasonable as it might be, slipped to another part of her history. She found a place in Jericho where her cousin lived and got a job as a maid in Worcester College.

'Wake up!' Caradog shouted at himself and for a time was back in his own body in the reality he accepted.

He lay back down on the bed and soon found himself listening to the sounds of the college kitchens. The clatter of the plates and swooshes of the sink-pumps, the orders from the men, the giggles from the women. This was not the sound of his college but those of Worcester College. Mary had slipped into his mind once more and he was returned to her haunting. All seemed well enough for a while then the proctors and the bulldogs started to use her as if it were their right.

Slip and slip again. She taught him what it was like to be a poor but fine-looking girl amongst the comfortable lives of the privileged. After yet more awful encounters, she left the college and its privilege because she reckoned that she could make better money selling that very thing that they kept taking from her.

He opened his eyes as he heard her voice.

'That's when I changed my name to Jaqueline.'

The following day he wandered as wraith-like as his masters, paying no attention to his surroundings but becoming every one of his victims in turn. A young man studying for the ministry, Heaven preserve us—the very young man who had been in the lecture hall! They were stepping back into the world of the living. All of them—a middle-aged banker's wife, a child, God help him, and a hundred more, each clamouring for attention, each hating him for dragging their souls into the maw of the Greyfriars.

'My God, my God!' he screamed as a dark caped figure reached for him out of the mist with fearsome blades on his fingers. Then those blades slashed his throat and he could scream no more. He began shaking as the blood was sucked from him and he remembered his whole life. Becoming a dissenter, Mansfield College, sacraments, studying of the Bible. The dedication to a life of service. A life that was ebbing away into the black distance where the Grimfriars waited in the ruins of an abbey.

Caradog returned to find that he was sitting beside the languid clay-filled water of the Cherwell. Why was this happening? Why, after all these years, was he losing control? Would the Grimfriars be able to help him? He thought not. He was simply a vessel to them—a conduit of blood and spirit from this world to theirs. God helps those who help themselves. He laughed at the thought. God wasn't going to help, was He? Yet perhaps the meaning could be adjusted to Fate helps those who help themselves. There had to be some stratagem to reverse these fearsome changes. What would Sherlock Holmes do?

He would wait until he had all the facts and then confront the perpetrator.

That was a place to start. Caradog went to the Bodleian Library and began his research. Old tomes in the Duke Humphries Library might provide some answers. Through the catalogues he pursued the theme. Amongst the dark shelves, he browsed. Through history he wandered, flighty as the dust illuminated by shafts of light through the gothic windows, Elen of the Ways always leading, her lantern illuminating a little of the path. She had been Magnus Maximus' wife, the woman for whom he had built the roads of Britain. She had been with him when he led his British army to take Rome but had left him before the last battle.

'I will not watch you die,' she had said.

And again. 'Your blood will stain the earth but I will not see it.'

Once she had left to return to The Isles of the Britons and the battle lost, Caradog found himself retreating with the remnants of the army through the Caucasian mountains. It was as true as if he was there. He had sword wounds, his feet were bleeding, his heart was broken at the bloody loss of his mighty captain.

Over the next five hundred years he grew into the blood-beast, living in the forests, becoming wilder with each taking of blood. The human in him slept until some part of it woke amongst the Bogomils, hating all that was constrained by the flesh. Hating blood. Hating desire.

There were times when he pondered his own hatred. This wasn't of his own mind, this disgust he held towards his physical self was imposed upon him by the others. He had been indoctrinated from birth, told that his own birth was a curse, that his parents were cursed and that only by self-hatred could he become eternal.

This wasn't real. This wasn't a way forward. God himself had surely become flesh in their lord, Jesus Christ.

'Not so,' replied the leaders of the order. 'Christ was pure spirit.'

The argument was absolute in their minds. It had to be, lest their whole edifice should fall and their reason turned to ruin.

They were like drowning men, clinging to a spar of their broken ship.

Drowning but not lacking in distorted perception and the malice that ran by its side, like a snarling war-dog. They tried to beat him into alignment with their will but each blow of the whip reinforced his doubt. He remained silent as they left him to bleed upon the Bosnian sand.

This Caradog in the previous millennium, discussed these matters with his ancient self, surrounded by earth stained with his own blood. Perhaps the flesh was not of the essence of God but Christ had shown that the blood was sacred. It was in both the writing and the sound; *Sang Real, San Greal*. Royal Blood, Holy Vessel. He would become the holy vessel of the holy blood and he would teach the world. Into the wilderness he went, alone and unfulfilled.

As the years of his life were counted, he no longer required the fleshy shell, only the blood that would be provided by those of lesser will, of lesser significance.

He stood alone as the first of the new order.

For a thousand years he stared into his own face, contemplating the contemplator. When he walked out into the bright sunlight, past the stone philosophers' heads of the Sheldonian and into the Broad, Caradog already knew what had to be done.

In the centre of the road by Trinity College, he paused to look at the cross, set firm and unmoving in the fabric of the thoroughfare, beneath the shuffling footsteps and rolling cart-wheels. This was the exact place that the martyrs had met their awful end, their blood boiling to the sky, their flesh dusted into the wind.

He thanked them for the memory they had given the world. Their God and the flesh He had created were about to be reunited in the name of all the martyrs. The world had changed. He was no longer moving from day to similar day, performing his duties, he was moving from one condition to another. He was a pilgrim with a perceived destination.

The clarity that derives from being close and considerate towards death was upon him. Back in his rooms, he bathed with extra care and similar consideration to his living self. The relationship between flesh and spirit was never more evident to him as he prepared to meet those that would divide the two. Caradog baptised himself in his own name.

That evening, at Godstow, standing upon the bones of a thousand pilgrims, he confronted the line of Grimfriars.

'Understanding has been given to me because I am the Elder,' he said.

They dismissed such a pompous notion. 'You are flesh,' they replied.

'I have been reborn.' He smiled at their unseen, unseeable faces under each hood in turn. 'My terms have changed. I am no longer your servant.'

He turned as he heard the sound of the bellows and the roar of the quickening brazier. Lesser thralls were heating the branding iron. In the increased light from the fire and the swirling sparks, he could see that another glass tube and tap were laid out on a cloth and before any of the grey figures spoke, he realised their significance. From their hollow faces they intoned 'You are therefore no longer able to carry out your duties. We cannot allow your flesh to continue.'

However, he was stronger than any of them and prepared for battle. Magnus' army, in which he had fought, flanked him and stood at his rear. The line of cornua howled and blasted, war drums mimicked the rising heartbeat and with a stamping of feet and roar of defiance, they carried him forward and away through the cowering enemy, pushing them hither and thither to burst out of the circle and run back past the lock towards the distant city, hearing the screaming of the next Blood-catcher as the iron was applied to him.

Alone again, out of breath, but feeling that he had escaped, Caradog slowed to a lope, but how do you outrun a wraith? The Hellish crew followed him in the mist from his heels and somewhere close to the ancient crossing of the Thames, they surrounded him. He looked at the hooded Grimfriars, towering over every one of those he had sacrificed to them and knew that his life was over. For with them was the recently signified Blood-letter, naked to the waist and showing the newly branded badge of office on his left breast. Caradog could smell that burned flesh mingling with the burning human fat of the candles carried by the regrouping army of thralls.

And pushing her way to the front came the lost waif Jaqueline, once so pretty, now so deathly. She smiled for the first time in years.

'Take comfort that those you imprisoned in your blood are now released.'

'And so am I,' he replied, then sighed as she had done.

***

The day after the professor's funeral, a dapper middle-aged man presented himself at the admission clerk's office of Saint John's College.

'Good morning. I am Professor Richard Meredith of Trinity College Cambridge and I understand that there is a vacancy in The History Faculty. May I present my certificates of qualification?'

Doggone

S.L. Markham

Every kid at some point asks their parents for a dog; Elliot was no different. Although, unlike most kids, he got what he asked for. On his 11th birthday, his mother told him his gift awaited him in the back garden. Rushing outside, he met a glamorous dog with an abundant mane and frill.

'Her name's Lily; she's a Rough Collie.'

Elliot almost didn't hear his mother, too busy petting Lily's dense coat as she panted happily.

'Hi, Lily! I'm Elliot.'

Lily huffed in his face in response. He made a face at her foul breath.

'She used to belong to Miss Anderson; you remember her?' his mother asked, giving Lily a few pets herself. Elliot frowned.

He did remember her, but not fondly. She was a bitter old lady who always sneered at him whenever he went by her house to get to school. Although Elliot counted himself lucky, that's all she did to him. Elliot's friend from school, Caleb, accidentally kicked his football into Miss Anderson's front garden while they were playing. When he hopped the fence to get it back, Miss Anderson appeared out of nowhere and started grabbing him while screaming nonsense. Elliot immediately rushed inside and got Caleb's parents to stop her; it was a good thing Elliot did because when they returned, Miss Anderson had started strangling the boy. He didn't know she had a dog.

Elliot couldn't imagine someone like her having a dog or, at the very least, treating it well. He nodded at his mother; she smiled sadly before speaking. 'Ah, well, she went to the hospital yesterday.'

'What happened?' he asked.

His mother looked away, 'Oh, y'know, she's old and not in her right mind half the time.'

More like all the time, thought Elliot.

His mother looked back at him with a smile, 'But! She left this poor girl behind, and since you've been driving me crazy about wanting a dog, I thought we could keep her. Until Miss Anderson gets better, at least, but who knows.' She pulls her son and the dog closer to her. 'Maybe if we do a good job, Miss Anderson will let us keep her.'

Elliot nodded, grinning, but one thing was bothering him. 'What about Delilah? Wouldn't she want Lily?'

His mother's smile wavered, 'We ... weren't able to contact her.'

Elliot sighed in dismay; he missed his old babysitter. She skipped town when she turned 18, and nobody'd seen her since. He couldn't blame her; if his mum were anything like Miss Anderson, he'd want to get away as soon as possible. But still, he wished she'd said goodbye first.

'Aw, sweetie, I'm sorry,' she kissed him on the forehead, 'I'm sure she'll come back someday.'

Elliot shrugged and scratched Lily behind the ears as she rested her head on his knee. After a minute, his mum stood up, wiping the grass stains from her legs.

'Well! I should get everything set up before our guests arrive.'

Elliot had almost forgotten about his party. 'Do you need any help, mum?'

She gave a dismissive wave of her hand, 'Go play with Lily; I'll call you when your friends arrive.'

Happily obeying his mother's order, Elliot found a big stick and threw it, thinking Lily would grab it; she did not. She, instead, stood there, staring up at him with unblinking dark brown eyes, stock still. It was a little eerie. For a moment, she looked like a taxidermised animal rather than a living creature. The illusion shattered as Lily quizzically tilted her head at him, and Elliot huffed out a laugh, feeling a little silly for getting spooked over a cute dog. Before he could explain the intricacies of fetch to the confused canine, his mother called out his name from the back porch. The guests had arrived. Lily had to stay outside in the garden since his mother said the amount of people and loud noises would stress her out since she's not used to it. Elliot understood, although he was disappointed that he couldn't introduce her to his friends. Even then, the party went off without a hitch. Several of his friends showed up—including Caleb—holding gifts likely bought by their parents.

The kids were halfway through an intense game of Go Fish when Elliot let slip about Lily

'Miss Anderson has a dog?' Olivia raised an eyebrow.

'I thought Lily was her kid?' Liam questioned.

'No stupid, that's Delilah.'

'Ohh.'

'Well, I hope Miss Anderson kicks it so you can keep her,' Caleb stated, 'She's horrible.'

The kids mumbled in agreement when Elliot's mother called them for cake. Before he knew it, the party had ended, and he waved his friends goodbye.

Lily shuffled back inside when his mother said it was time for bed. Birthday or not, he still had school tomorrow. So Elliot bid Lily and his mother goodnight and headed to his room to change and slip into his bed. As soon as his head hit the pillow, he was out like a light.

Elliot probably would have slept until his alarm went off if the sound of muffled sobbing didn't wake him. He sleepily rubbed his eyes as he turned to look at his alarm clock. 11:55 PM, the bright red numbers stared back at him. He carefully climbed out of bed and tiptoed to his closed bedroom door, carefully opening it. Now that the door was open, he could hear the sobbing more clearly; it was coming from downstairs. Was his mother crying? Did she hurt herself?

Elliot headed downstairs and crept through the dark towards the sound of heavy sobbing. He'd crossed the threshold of the kitchen when he gasped at what he saw; illuminated by the moonlight from the window was the sight of a familiar figure sitting on the floor.

It was Delilah, except the Delilah he knew had long hair, dyed different shades of pink, with bright eyes and band shirts he was too young to listen to. The Delilah in front of him had a shaved head with a few tufts of black hair spared, distant eyes glassy with tears and a threadbare shirt barely hiding her skeletal frame.

The worst part was the bunched-up fur around Delilah's legs. At first, he assumed it was some sort of furred coat, but as he looked closer, he realised it wasn't a coat. It was the deflated form of a Rough Collie; Lily looked like a bearskin rug.

Deathtrap

Jarick Weldon

Crunch, flop, crunch, flop.

'Can't you just walk on the sleepers, Carver?' Jack Elliot asked, pointing his torch forwards as they walked through the murky railway tunnel. 'If you keep going on the gravel like that, I'll break your fucking knees and leave you here.' Jack cast an imposing figure in the dark, more so when contrasted with his wiry companion. His black coat was stretched across ripped muscles. He wasn't the kind of man who went to the gym in nylon shorts. His training regimen was fists to punching bag, inanimate or otherwise.

'Sorry, mate,' Charlie replied, his thin, miserable face like the Ghost of Christmas I Didn't Get Any Presents.

'We've been in here too long.'

Flop, flop, flop, flop, crunch.

'For Christ—,' Jack began again, before deciding to rein in his frustration before it became a full stampede. Carver's footsteps weren't the only noises in the tunnel. Plops and splats echoed as oversized water drops from the arched roof hit the tracks. Puddles changed the flops and crunches into slaps and sploshes. Rats scuttled into the darkness with squeaks and chattering, no doubt having conversations about the two intruders in their domain. *Smart creatures, rats, but creepy as shit*, Jack thought. He didn't like the tunnel, not at all.

What seemed like hours ago, Carver had called out, but the only replies were his echoes: 'HELLO! ... Hello! ... Hello ... hello ...' He had a high-pitched voice, matching his frame and attitude. Jack had hissed at him to shut his bloody trap. Since then, they'd walked mostly in silence, apart from the flops and plops, sploshes and squeaks, and occasional, mostly one-way exchanges about who was at fault for their predicament. Jack knew exactly who was to blame: Charlie Carver. *I'll reckon with him later*, he thought, re-running the earlier events in his mind.

***

Jack thought he had made a good plan, but its fabric had quickly unravelled, like a charity store blanket attacked by giant moths.

The Eight Until Late grocers and off-license was in the middle of a row of rough concrete units. It was well past the second Eight, and comfortably into the realms of Late. A drenching rain had driven other ne'er do wells from the street. Fluorescent lights beamed out from the store into the darkness, as if saying: 'Please rob me.' Jack intended to oblige. There were three other shops in the row, all closed for the night: a bookmaker where the poor went to get poorer, a sandwich takeaway under special measures after an incident with some tuna mayo, and a charity store missing only a moth-eaten blanket from its repertoire of junk.

Jack had brought Charlie Carver along to drive. Carver wasn't too bright, but he was a friend of Jasmine's sister. He had form and a gun. Jack would do anything for Jasmine. She was his scented flower. He thought back to her parting words as he left. 'Get me some gin you dickhead, and don't get fucking caught,' she'd said.

The rainwater had defeated the drains and was flowing under their car like a miniature river, complete with rapids. Carver had boasted about the black two-seater he'd brought. Jack was unconvinced: 'And this is MOTed?'

'I dunno, mate. I nicked it, didn't I.'

'What I'm saying is, it looks like a piece of shit. Must be twenty years old.'

'Well, it didn't have a working alarm.'

'That should've told you something.'

They pulled woollen balaclavas over their heads. Jack pushed open the shop door. He'd planned the job as a straightforward in and out to grab the till contents and some higher-end booze, including at least one bottle of gin. But grey-haired fate had other ideas.

Ding, ding.

There was a scrawny youth standing behind the counter, wearing an orange apron scrawled in just legible writing with 'Eight Until Late.' Only one customer stood at the counter, a wrinkled, grey-haired woman with a dripping umbrella in one hand and a bottle of sherry in the other. Both occupants turned towards the robbers.

Jack opened negotiations. 'Keep your fucking hands in sight. This gun's real. No messing. Money from the till now.' His tactic was always to scare first, to eliminate any thoughts of resistance.

Charlie added, in a squeal, waving his own gun: 'Do what he says!'

The grey-haired woman yelled and charged at them, umbrella pointing, sherry bottle raised. Jack saw the rest of the events in a state of surprised slow motion.

'Whoa' Charlie said, taking a step backwards and bumping into the door. His finger squeezed.

Bang.

A splash of red flew from the side of the woman's neck, and she span like a figure skater on replay. Scarlet blood Jackson Pollocked the wall. The bottle slipped from her fingers and smashed. She fell to the ground, gurgling into a pool of sherry.

'You idiot,' Jack shouted at Carver. 'Out, now!'

They legged it to the car. Charlie floored the accelerator. 'Shit, shit, shit!' The wheels spun, spraying a curtain of water across the pavement. Jack remembered they had driven off into the darkness, windscreen wipers flapping erratically against the torrent of rain.

***

Flop, flop, flop, flop.

Jack shuddered. The torchlight flickered. He wanted to blank out the events. He wasn't' sure he could remember it all anyway. *PTSD, probably*, he thought. Carver had driven at speed. Behind them, blue flashing lights appeared in the mirrors, haloed in the downpour. They must have abandoned the car before escaping.

'This way,' Charlie had said. 'Here, into the tunnel. It's too late for trains now. We can get through to the other side.'

***

Flop, flop, ... flop, flop.

The tunnel continued straight ahead with no gradient. Beyond the reach of the torchlight, there was only darkness. Carver's earlier episode of shouting had apparently drawn no pursuers. Jack wondered how long they'd been in the tunnel. He seemed to have lost all track of time. Jasmine would be wondering where he was, and her gin.

Flop, ... flop, flop, ... flop.

'Do you think she's dead?' Charlie asked, not for the first time.

'What do you think, with that fucking great hole in her neck?'

They lapsed back into silence, walking slower now. The torchlight was weaker. Jack could only see two railway sleepers ahead.

Flop ... flop ... flop ...

'Shush,' Charlie whispered.

They both stood still.

Flop ... ... flop.

'The footsteps. They haven't stopped—' Jack said.

Flop.

'Shush! Listen!' Charlie insisted.

Then, Jack heard it. A low rumble, a distant rattling. He felt a breath of cold damp air.

'No, that can't be right,' Charlie said, nervously.

A light was coming towards them, getting brighter, quickly.

'Shit! Shit!' Charlie yelled.

'Shit! ... Shit ... shit ... shit,' the tunnel squealed back, before a whoosh of frozen air, a thundering wail, grinding metal on metal, and the blazing light reached them.

'Aaah!!'

'Shit!!'

Silence.

Darkness.

***

'Nope, mine's gone,' said the paramedic.

'Yeah, mine too,' said his colleague.

'Thirty-five minutes of CPR. I wondered with those last few heartbeats if we might just get this one back.'

'I broke a few ribs on my guy at the beginning. Heard them go crunch. Can't say we didn't try our best, though. Even with what they did.'

'Let's call it, then.'

They stepped back from the two bodies lying by the mangled two-seater.

'Not the best getaway car to have chosen in this weather. A deathtrap, really.'

Blue lights flashed around them in the pouring rain.

Scrooge's Chain

Kathy Goddard

Roland Lennox allowed himself a sigh of contentment as he sank into the red leather wing-backed chair. It had cost him a pretty penny, he couldn't deny it, but as soon as he had spotted it in the window display of a fashionable shop, he wanted it—and what Roland wanted, Roland got.

The chair was comfortable, and he spent many a happy hour sitting in this, his favourite room, in a chair moulded over years of use to the shape of his buttocks. The room had been decorated to his exact specifications, from the soft cream walls and dark oak bookshelves which lined three walls, to the framed landscapes on either side of the fireplace. Strewn about the polished floorboards were several expensive rugs. Gave the place an extra touch of class, he thought.

Relaxing into the back of the chair, Roland drew deeply on his fat cigar, squinting as he watched the blue smoke drift towards the ceiling. An old black and white version of *A Christmas Carol* flickered on his television screen. He used to know most of the actors, but these days it was harder to grasp those memories; as difficult to catch hold of as his cigar smoke. He did recognise Alastair Sim though, as the despicable Scrooge.

Roland had only vague recollections of moving to this house but, having reached the age of ninety-two and outliving most of his contemporaries, the odd lapse in his memory was forgivable.

Heaving himself out of the chair with a grunt he picked his way carefully across the room, so as not to trip over any of the rugs and risk a broken ankle. His old bones would not heal so quickly as in his youth.

Standing before the ornately framed mirror, he surveyed his image. The glass surface had tarnished over the years, whereas he had aged with relatively blemish-free skin and fewer wrinkles than a man of his age should expect. Running a hand over his bald pate, he briefly mourned the loss of his hair; thick, black and glossy, reminiscent of a young Elvis, but it had started to thin more than half a century ago.

A trick of the light showed him a brief image of himself as that young man; bold and brash, with a full head of Brylcreemed hair. He hadn't been Roland then, of course. He had reinvented himself more than once in order to escape the circumstances of his birth in the slums of the city.

'And I did it too,' he told his reflection. 'With no help from anyone, I fought my way out of that life.'

No help from anyone? That's not exactly true, is it?

The thought leapt into his mind as clearly as if someone had whispered it into his ear. He shook his head as if to dislodge the notion. Of course he had done it alone. He had relied on himself at all times. He had never needed others. He might have used them for a while as he ascended the ranks of society, but had discarded them as soon as they had helped him to achieve his goal. They had helped him to gain his lofty position, but could never have hoped to climb by his side. There it was. No harm done.

No harm? Do you really believe that?

Where were these thoughts coming from? They were so clear that he could detect a mocking tone underlying the words. His mind had never played such tricks on him before. He made a mental note to consult his private doctor.

Returning to his chair, he settled into its comforting embrace. The film flickered on; the ghost of Christmas past making its appearance. Hang on, this wasn't right. The ghost was played by a man; he was certain of it, not a young, undeniably beautiful woman, shot in soft focus. She looked vaguely familiar, but there had been so many women throughout the years that he couldn't possibly be expected to remember them all. What was so special about this one? Why did he get the feeling he had known her? These memory lapses were unsettling.

He leaned closer to the screen, peering at it in the fading light. As he stared, the limpid eyes grew sharper, pinning him like a butterfly in a collector's display cabinet. The cheekbones became more pronounced and the woman's lips pulled back into a tight rictus grin. As he watched, flesh and hair dissolved to reveal the skull beneath. He shrieked and pushed himself back into his chair. When he looked again, the ghost was once more played by a man.

Roland was shaken. Pushing himself upright once more, he headed for the sideboard where a cut-glass decanter of whisky awaited him. He lifted it from the silver tray and poured himself a dram, gulping it down and, even as he coughed and spluttered, he poured another. He hesitated and then picked up the decanter in case he decided another refill was necessary.

The film had unsettled him and he didn't want to watch any more. He switched the television off and sank into the depths of his chair.

Out of sight, out of mind, eh Billy?

Billy? No one had called him Billy since he had left the slums more than seventy years ago. Several incarnations ago. This thought had come with a different voice—a woman's. The earlier intrusive voice had been male, he was certain of it. Both sounded familiar, though he couldn't place them. Faint echoes from a distant past, perhaps. He shrugged. Did it matter? No.

Nevertheless, as he clutched his glass, his thoughts re-wound like cine film to his youth. Despite the lack of encouragement from his parents, he had been a natural scholar, spurning friendships in order to study and gain a coveted scholarship to a good school. Being a scholarship boy, however, did not endear him to his peers. Spineless rich boys, who were there due to their fathers' fat wallets rather than their academic prowess, looked down on him and rejected him. One boy in particular had irritated him. What was his name now? James? John? Something like that. No ... Jeremy. That was it! Not so much wrong with the memory after all.

That's right—Jeremy. Good, you're remembering.

Roland twisted round. The male voice was back, and had hissed the words into his left ear. He took another mouthful of whisky, gasping as it burned his throat. Jeremy had been everything that Roland had despised—or was it everything that he had wanted to be himself? Tall, blond, rich. He and Roland had played tricks on each other in a cat and mouse game of one-upmanship. Boyish games, that's all they were.

Games? You dare to call them GAMES?

The hiss became a shout and the cut glass tumbler slipped from his fingers. Missing the rug, it shattered on the wooden floor, shards glistening at his feet like newly shed tears. The air around him shimmered, reminding him of heat haze on damp roads warmed by the sun.

He had drunk his whisky too quickly, that was all. It had rushed to his head, leaving him muddled and too lethargic to push himself out of his chair. A malaise had stolen over him, draining him of energy. He cast nervous glances at the television set. He couldn't rid himself of that woman's image, even though his thoughts were now directed elsewhere.

He hadn't thought about Jeremy for years but now he was inundated by memories of boys studying, playing rugby or clamouring for extra pudding in the refectory. He sniffed as if the aroma of overcooked vegetables and sweaty adolescent boys could still be detected. In his first year, Roland had struggled. He had been unable to break into their cliques, but at the beginning of his second year he had gained their grudging respect, having unmasked one of their own as a thief. Jeremy. Roland wondered what had happened to him. He had been expelled, of course. Served him right.

Served me right?

The voice was now a shriek and Roland put his hands up to cover his ears.

That won't help.

The voice spoke the truth. This wasn't an external voice after all; this must be coming from inside his head. His conscience?

Conscience? You have no conscience. You still can't admit the truth to yourself, even after all these years.

'What truth?'

Roland's voice cracked. What was he doing? Talking to himself, that's what. Definitely time to speak to his doctor. Expensive, but worth every grudged penny.

Think, Billy boy!

This was an order. Too scared to disobey, he forced his thoughts back to his school days. He saw himself, as if watching a film, sneaking into bedrooms, taking items of value; watches, wallets, silver bedside clocks, placing them into a shoebox and sliding it under Jeremy's bed. He had blocked this, along with other misdemeanours, from his mind as the years passed, but now his life was laid before him and various incidents unfolded—lies, manipulation and downright bullying. So he hadn't been—he wasn't—a nice man. So what?

Are you remembering?

'You.'

Are you sorry?

'Hell, no!' Roland roared. 'I did what it took to get where I am. No one else would have helped me, so I had to rely on myself. No, I have no regrets.

What about those you hurt?

'They were the sort to land on their feet. No real harm done.'

What about Violet?

'Who?'

Of course, you introduced her as Verity. Forced her to change her name to suit you. Vi didn't suit your image.

Searching through the women in his memory, Roland finally located Violet, a shy young thing he had met when she was in her early twenties. He had tried to groom her, but she kept letting him down, giving herself away with her broad accent and lack of sophistication. He had no choice but to let her go.

But not until you had beaten her half to death!

Roland shifted in his chair. It was true that it had taken him a few years to learn how to control his temper, and yes, he might have given Violet one or two slaps. Everything shimmered as if the very air was angry with him.

It only took one blow to the stomach for Vi to lose her baby. Your baby.

'I have no children,' snapped Roland. It was the one, the only, disappointment in his life.

You could have had a son.

The woman's voice was heard again and he recognised the flattened vowels of those born, like him, in the slums.

'Verity? Is that you?'

VIOLET!

There was a click as the television set switched itself back on. Scrooge and his ghosts had disappeared, and white static crackled behind the glass, slowly clearing to reveal the figure of a beautiful, angry young woman.

'Was that you in the film?' he croaked.

Yes—as I was when you knew me.

But not how she looked when she died. When you killed her.

'But I didn't kill her. I didn't know she was pregnant and I didn't kill her. You're talking nonsense—I'm talking nonsense. It's just my mind playing tricks.'

Another figure materialised beside that of Violet, one which Roland recognised immediately. Jeremy. He looked just as Roland remembered him; tall blond, arrogant. Verity—Violet—was even more beautiful than he remembered, with long, dark, softly waved hair and deep blue eyes. She looked spectacular. It was such a shame that she had become a liability. She would have looked good on his arm. Oh well. It didn't matter. His mind had conjured them a result of his age and his whisky, nothing more.

Do you want to know what happened to me? Look!

Jeremy again.

Roland didn't know and didn't care. He closed his eyes and leaned against the chair's wing, refusing to play along with his mind's nonsense.

I said LOOK!

The television burst into vibrant colour. Roland's head shot forward and, however much he endeavoured to keep them closed, his eyes opened, fixed on the image of his schoolboy foe, incongruous amongst the Dickensian actors now milling around in the background. Jeremy, tall, well-built and athletic, dissolved on the screen before him, to be replaced by a thin, haunted youth, his eyes and teeth too big for his shrunken face, his stick thin legs looking too fragile to hold his slight weight. Roland was unable to force his gaze away from that sharp face which slowly morphed into that of a monster with bulging eyes and a protruding tongue, ligature marks livid around his throat.

I was 19. Thrown out by my parents for disgracing them. None of my so-called friends would take me in. I was beaten up by every member of the rugby team, did you know that?

'I didn't know. I'm ... sorry.'

Sorry isn't enough. I had nowhere to go. You went from strength to strength and I ... died.

'Not my fault,' muttered Roland. 'Not my fault.'

He tried to push himself upright and escape these thoughts but was unable to move, as if pinned down by a heavy weight. His eyes swivelled as he looked for a way to escape from this room, which was now more a prison than a sanctuary. A prison with sadistic warders.

I died too, Billy. After I lost my baby, I didn't care about anything. Not myself, not my family, not you. I was in a permanent daze, wandering the streets, not eating or drinking. I worried about my son not having a grave, so I went to graveyards to try and see where he should have gone, but the first cold night caught me out. I died and I was glad.

Violet reappeared on his screen. Like Jeremy, her good looks faded, her skin slid from her skull, leaving bare patches amongst the once lustrous hair. Her eyes, even as they sank back into their orbits, never stopped glaring at him.

A sharp pain blossomed in Roland's chest. He clutched at it as he doubled over. Was this how his life was going to end? A heart attack, brought on by memories of his alleged past misdeeds?

'Help me,' he croaked.

Did you help us?

Let's leave him. Let him suffer like we suffered …

'Verity? You were always kind … help me …'

Verity? That's a laugh. Means honest, don't it? You were never honest! I'm Violet!

Roland groaned. His only conscious thought was that if he died, at least the pain would stop. Unexpected laughter echoed around him and he looked up to see the ruined figures of Jeremy and Violet pointing at him and giggling like schoolchildren.

You don't get it, do you, Roland? You're not going to die—you can't die.

Jeremy and Violet reached out from the television screen and pulled him into the film itself. His thin slippers offered little protection and were quickly soaked, leaving him shivering in the snow covered street. Violet placed a hand upon his shoulder and turned him round. Roland found himself looking back through the glass at his room.

Just look at yourself—Roland Lennox, self-made, successful business man.

Jeremy. Still taunting him, even in the afterlife. Whose afterlife? Roland looked out and saw his body, hunched and shrivelled in his chair, mummified fingers clutching at the fabric of his dressing gown.

'Am—am I dead?'

Too right you are! Welcome to your hell! Forget Scrooge's chain, this is the hell you created for yourself—no one cared enough to come and find you—just like they won't come tomorrow, or next week or next month … there's only us. Violet and I found each other and now we've found you.

Behind them Scrooge was screeching as the ghost of Christmas future led him to a graveyard and pointed out his own tombstone.

'Why are you doing this? What do you want?'

Roland may have been frightened but his overriding emotion was anger. How dare they treat him like this!

We want revenge, Billy boy! What else? Unlike Scrooge back there, you've shown no remorse for your sins, so you are still accountable. But let's take the Scrooge analogy one step further, shall we? People forget get that there were actually more than three ghosts in A Christmas Carol, weren't there Violet?

Verity's laugh rang out as clearly as the church bells that were pealing in celebration of Christmas Day.

Oh yes—there were four ghosts—Past, Present, Future and the ghost of Jacob Marley.

'So what? You're talking nonsense—you two are the only ghosts here, if that's what you are. I still don't believe in you. You're nothing but imagination and whisky!'

You make three, Billy boy!

'Still not enough! Ha! Even in death I'm smarter than the two of you! No wonder I was the one who succeeded. You two just gave up.'

You haven't met the fourth yet …

Something was moving in the bundle Verity was holding. As Roland looked on in horror a tiny skeletal arm emerged. The fingers shifted as if they were waving at him. Violet pulled the blanket open to reveal the child she was cradling, its spine bent and its skull dented. Dark blue eyes, full of accusation, were fixed on him.

In the background Scrooge was merrily buying the largest turkey, but Roland couldn't look away from the grotesque figure.

Meet your son, Roland. Isn't he beautiful? Here, do you want to hold him? Isn't he the best Christmas present ever?

As the child was held aloft Roland shrieked and tried to twist away, but Jeremy held him in place. As the shrivelled fingers reached out to touch his cheek, Roland welcomed the darkness that closed in as swiftly as a bat's wings around a moth. As he lost consciousness he felt himself being pulled back into his room. He fell onto his chair, their mocking words echoing around the room:

See you tomorrow, Billy boy, when we can play this game all over again.

The Black Sheep

Michael Noonan

When Percy Clarence Manderville unexpectedly inherited Murcombe Manor he thought that it was the best free gift that he had ever been given. But he didn't realise at the time that it came with certain strings attached and that it wasn't going to pan out to be anything like the undiluted blessing he envisaged it to be.

His father, now deceased, was the only brother of the bachelor Earl of Murcombe. When the Earl recently died in a tragic accident, after being thrown from his horse, Percy found himself—being the only offspring of his father—the heir to the vast property of Murcombe Manor.

Though the only nephew of the late Earl, there had been precious little contact between the two of them during the Earl's life. A bitter family feud between the two brothers—together with the late Earl regarding young Percy as an out-and-out bounder and reprobate, and a disgrace to the family name—had meant that their relationship was practically non-existent. Indeed, the late Earl had contemplated drawing up a new will with the express purpose of disinheriting Percy altogether and handing his estate to a more distant relation. But he had deferred it, feeling that there was no real urgency in the matter, as he was convinced that he had a good few years in him yet.

Percy's father had seldom mentioned his brother at all, except in the most negative and disparaging terms, and had rarely reminisced, in Percy's presence, about his early life at the Manor. Thus in a real sense the new Earl was as much a stranger to his new home as any passing Japanese or American tourist. Still, he intended to make the most of his sudden windfall. And felt indeed as if he had won the jackpot on the Lottery.

***

'Will that be all, M'lord?' said the butler, Melchett, as he delivered the tea and muffins, along with an ironed newspaper for his Lordship to scrutinise.

'Now that you mention it, Melchett, there is something I've been meaning to raise with you.'

'Indeed.'

'I want to have a new bedroom prepared, in the East Wing. I've noticed you get a better view of the grounds from that end of the house.'

At that unexpected request the colour seemed to drain from Melchett's mask-like face and alarm was evident in his eyes.

'Anything wrong?'

'I'm afraid your Lordship that such a request is quite out of the question. No one is allowed to stop overnight in the East Wing. Before midnight we lock all access doors to that wing. They aren't opened again till morning. That has always been the case as long as I've been here. And well before.'

The new Earl of Murcombe stared with incredulity at the sober, diminutive figure of the butler. 'Are you quite serious about this, Melchett?'

'Indeed I am, sir.'

Sat nearby, Reginald Rigby—the louche, slovenly dressed companion of his Lordship; with a pony tail and scraggy beard—also looked on with curious bemusement; those intriguing comments having distracted him from the game of patience he had been playing with a deck of cards.

'And what's all that in aid of?' asked Rigby.

Melchett glanced briefly at Rigby with barely suppressed contempt, before turning back to Lord Manderville. The whole crew he heartily detested; and in particular the new Earl of Murcombe Manor. He could have been, like his late Uncle, a presentable looking man, who took a pride in his appearance, if he put his mind to it. Instead, to Melchett, he seemed like a down-and-out; with his long, greasy hair, unshaven chin, his crumpled trousers, torn, denim jacket, festooned with badges, and the rings in his ears. On top of all that there was his Lordship's shady background, prior to taking possession of the estate. He was a University drop-out with a string of drug offences to his name, and who had seen the inside of a few prisons. He'd spent the best part of the previous decade out in the Far East, and, according to some press reports, allegedly making a living from such illicit and unsavoury occupations as pimping, drug pushing, and even arms smuggling. While the rest of them, Mandeville's blonde girl-friend, Reginald Rigby and his Filipino wife, were hardly more congenial to the Butler's rigorous, conservative tastes. But, his was not to reason why.

'Perhaps I should have explained the situation earlier to you, your Lordship. There are, how should I put it; disturbances and manifestations, of a particularly paranormal nature, which are known to occur, after midnight and before dawn, on that very wing of the Manor.'

'You mean we have a haunted house here?' exclaimed Manderville.

'Only on the East Wing, your Lordship. And only after midnight.'

'A ghost,' said Rigby. 'I don't know if I like the sound of that?'

'Has nobody ever stopped there after midnight?' asked the Earl.

'One rather foolish journalist persuaded his late Lordship, against his better judgment, to allow him to stay the night on the East Wing, over fifteen years ago.'

'Yeah. And what happened?'

'He died of a heart attack.'

The Earl and Rigby looked at each other for a second.

'And have you any idea what, or who, could be the cause of this haunting?' asked the Earl.

'We believe, indeed, we are convinced, that it is an early ancestor of yours, your Lordship.'

***

The next day Lord Manderville raised the subject with the estate manager, Charles Bidewell—a solid, phlegmatic man in his fifties—and the last person one would suspect of harbouring casual supernatural beliefs.

'Oh, it's absolutely true; there's no doubt about it,' came the astonishing reply. 'The East Wing is haunted. Has been for generations past. No one in their right mind would spend a night there beyond midnight. I can vouch for that,' and then with a note of disdain which he couldn't entirely censor from his voice, 'your Lordship.'

'Melchett says it's the ghost of some early ancestor of mine?'

'Yes, it is indeed.'

'Which one?'

'It's undoubtedly the ghost of the Seventh Earl.'

'The Seventh Earl!' said his Lordship, reflectively. 'Ah yes. My old man did mention him a time or two, as I recall.'

'Before the decision was made to lock all the access doors to the East Wing, during the night hours,' said Bidewell, 'he was seen and heard by a number of servants. To their acute alarm and distress; as one might imagine.'

Lord Manderville nodded his head.

'And according to their testimony he bore a striking resemblance to the surviving pictures we have of the Seventh Earl.'

'And is he never seen at all during the daylight hours?'

'No. Only at night.'

'Y'know, I'd like to know a bit more about this ancestor of mine.'

'You'll find an informative chapter on him, your Lordship, in a history of the house written by a local antiquarian, the Reverend Foxglove. There's an old leather bound edition in the Manor's library.'

'Is there now.' He nodded his head. 'Thanks for letting me know. I'll certainly give it a perusal. It sounds as if he was a bit of a character?'

'Oh yes; he was straight out of the rogues' gallery. You should find him quite interesting.'

He went to the library, got hold of the book, took it over to a table, by a window, and turned to the relevant chapter, which went under the appropriate title: 'The Black Sheep'. He read on. The Seventh Earl had lived in the Eighteenth Century. On inheriting the Manor from his father he embarked on a life of debauchery and dissipation that was remarkable even for those profligate times. He ran through such hoards of money on the gaming tables of London that he almost bankrupted his estate and was forced to sell priceless paintings and treasures—some of them ending up as far away as Catherine the Great's Hermitage in St Petersburg—in order to salvage his property.

Aside from this he was known for his womanising, drunkenness and truculent behaviour. He thought of no one except himself. He cheated and lied to his associates, as a matter of course; badly treated his underlings—took frightful liberties with his younger female servants; and was a very byword for scandal. Yet there were even darker skeletons rattling in his closet. He had killed a man in a duel; brought about through his adamant refusal to pay off a gambling debt. There were stories of arcane, satanic rituals, and membership of the notorious Hell-Fire Club. And there was speculation that he may even have poisoned his first wife. A rumour that was only strengthened, when, after the briefest interval of grieving, he went on to marry his mistress. Even his own aristocratic caste all but washed their hands of him; and when his life of excess and debauchery caught up with him and he died of a sudden seizure in his fifties, there were precious few mourners. Rather, a sense of heart-felt relief.

Instead of being appalled by that sorry story of a rake's undoing, the new Earl rather warmed to that distant ancestor—as if he felt the presence of a kindred spirit from across the centuries. There were two illustrations of the wicked Earl. One, as a handsome young Georgian beau, dressed in all his finery—and the other; a grotesque, pock-marked, prematurely aged roué, bearing all the marks of his depravity on his bloated countenance, like the portrait of Dorian Grey.

That same afternoon he came across a full-length portrait of the nefarious Earl, in a hallway of the East Wing. It was of the younger, more attractive creature. There was a knowing, almost cynical smile on his face, and his eyes looked directly at the viewer, in a condescending and disdainful way. He seemed to Manderville to be someone who was confident and sure of himself, who would tread his own, distinct path through life, regardless of what others would say, and who would allow no one and nothing to get in his way.

He took the book out of the library and gave it to his girlfriend, Elaine. 'Just have a read of that chapter on the black sheep.'

Elaine was a tall, vivacious blonde, whose lively, colourful clothing could almost be described as psychedelic. She was a former university student who had dropped out of a Sociology course in the second year and went back packing with some girlfriends to the Far East. And it was three years ago when Mandeville first met her, while she was working as a lap dancer in a seedy bar in Hong Kong.

She read the chapter, then shook her head and smiled at Percy.

'What a monster.'

'At least he had a bit of life in him. Which is more than my uncle ever had.' He took the book from her hand. 'There's a rather striking portrait of him hanging in the East Wing, if you'd care to have a look at it, Elaine?'

'Sure.'

They walked over and stood before the painting.

'Wasn't a bad looking chap was he; before his life caught up with him?' She looked at the present Earl, with a wry smile on her lips. 'In fact he looks rather like you, Percy.'

'Is that an insult or a compliment?'

'Take it any way you like.' She paused. 'Yes, if you ignore the wig and the fancy costume, there is a definite resemblance.'

'Well, we are related,' he smiled.

'And look at that sly smile on his face. That's what you look like, Percy, when you've pulled some prank or practical joke.'

'Yes, we may well be kindred spirits.'

She looked at Manderville, knowingly. 'Well that wouldn't surprise me at at all.' She looked back at the portrait. 'D'you believe the story about the ghost, Percy?'

He shook his head. 'No. I'm afraid I'm a bit of a skeptic when it comes to matters like that, Elaine. It seems to me like a useful marketing gimmick to keep the coach-parties coming. After all, most of these old houses seem to have a convenient ghost or two knocking about. In fact you get the impression that if they didn't have one, they'd have to make one up.'

'So you think all that stuff about the East Wing is all made up?'

'Indeed. And I intend to show up this story for the fake I believe it to be.'

'Oh yeah.'

'I'm going to spend a night on the East Wing. And I'll rope in Rigby, for a bit of moral support.'

'He might not like it?'

'He has no choice in the matter.'

'But what will the butler say?'

'Who's going to tell him?'

'But you heard what he said? No one's allowed in the East Wing after midnight.'

'You know me by now, Elaine. When have I ever followed rules that other people had laid down? Besides; I'm the boss round here. I can do what the hell I like.' He shook his head as if to shake all the warnings he had heard out of his mind. 'No; that place isn't out of bounds as far as I'm concerned.'

'But what if this one is for real, Percy? What if there is a ghost?'

'I don't believe in all that supernatural malarkey. But even if such a thing did exist? Well, so what. From everything I've heard ghosts are quite insubstantial creatures. They don't seem to pack much of a punch. Why should I be concerned about something like that?' He smiled and waved a dismissive arm. 'I've probably seen worse things on a drug trip.'

An hour later his Lordship chanced upon Rigby in the billiard room, trying to pot a black.

'Rigby, old son; I've got a little adventure lined up for the two of us. Something a bit out of the ordinary.'

'Yeah,' muttered Rigby, looking up from the green baize.

'We're going to do a spot of ghost-hunting.'

'Yer don't say.'

***

The Earl had a commodious room fixed-up as a study, on the upper floor of the East Wing, for his daytime use. He then managed to purloin a key to one of the access doors, to the East Wing, while the butler was temporarily absent from the house, and had a copy made at a key-cutting stall in the market of a nearby town. He returned the original key to where he found it.

He made his plans, fixed a date and waited. At length the hour came. At one o'clock in the morning, when all the servants were fast asleep and the whole house was deserted and quiet, Lord Manderville unlocked an access door with his duplicate key and, together with Rigby, slipped into the dread East Wing.

They stealthily made their way up the stairs and along a hallway and came at length to the Earl's private room. The two adventurers had come well prepared for their long night's vigil. In the room, they had a television, together with a DVD player and a number of movie discs. There were several bottles of wine, that had been taken up from the cellars, a bottle of brandy, cans of lager, two packed lunches and a tin of assorted biscuits. And there were two sleeping bags, ready to unroll. Ghost or no ghost, they were determined to have a comfortable time. Though they kept the sound down, so as not to alert the rest of the house.

'Just imagine the looks on their faces, Rigby, when they find us here, fast asleep, tomorrow. It'll certainly have old Melchett in a flap.'

'It's not them I'm concerned about,' said Rigby as he poured some wine into a glass.

'You don't believe in all that guff about a ghost, d'you?'

'I don't know. But all this seems a damn fool idea to me.' He swallowed a measure of wine. 'After all, we don't know what we're dealing with.'

'It doesn't bother me.'

'But you heard what the butler said. A guy died of a heart attack who tried on the same caper we're pulling tonight.'

'If you ask me it was just a coincidence. People do die of heart attacks and seizures. I don't think it had anything to do with a ghost. You're taking this far too seriously, Rigby. You want to try and chill out a bit.'

***

A clock chimed two o'clock. Gusts of wind shook the windows and rainwater ran down the panes.

'Looks like we could be in for quite a downpour.'

'Yeah. Just the weather for a ghost,' reflected Rigby, as he recalled some of the old horror movies he had seen, where thunder, lightning and storms seemed almost obligatory. He drained off the contents of a brandy glass and then got to his feet. 'I'm off to the loo.'

'If you see anything spooky out there, let me know.'

'If I see anything like that I'll probably run a mile.'

There was an ominous rumble of thunder followed by a flash of lightning.

'Though I reckon your imagination can play tricks with you on a night like this,' Rigby reflected.

'Don't get yourself lost, Rigby. I know what you're like when you've been on the booze. And whatever else you've been taking.'

'I think I know my way around this place by now. And as for the booze? Well; there's no way that I'd be up here stone cold sober.'

'We're going to do a bit of exploring when you come back. We're going to see if there is anything to this ghost business. Though I can't help feeling that it's all a con job.'

'I'll be back. Don't worry. Though I still think this is a stupid escapade.' And with that he staggered off in the general direction of the loo.

Manderville lit a cigar and pulled the ring on a can of lager. He sat back and aimlessly leafed through a magazine, as without, the rain intensified and thunder rumbled in the heavens.

Ten minutes passed, but there was no sight or sound of Rigby. 'What's keeping him?' he mumbled to himself as he crushed the empty lager can and threw it in a wastepaper basket. 'I told him not to get lost.'

Five more minutes passed, and Rigby was still absent.

Rigby couldn't have left the East Wing, even if he wanted to. Manderville had locked the access door after they had entered the wing. And only he had the key.

'What a bore,' he groused; 'if he's gone and dossed down somewhere and left me here on my own tonight? Didn't I tell him to go easy on the booze?' Though he had drunk as much, if not more than his companion had. Despite his bluster and bravado he wasn't nearly as confident or bullish about that escapade as he had made out; and facing such a challenge on his own wasn't at all to his taste. He threw aside the magazine.

Another five minutes slipped by and Rigby was as evasive as ever. He reluctantly got to his feet and made his way over to the door. 'I'll have to blow him out,' he growled, as he walked along the hallway to the loo. By that time the storm was even more intensive; thunder growled overhead and flashes of lightning illuminated, fitfully, the gloomy apartments of the Manor.

He switched on a hall light, but the bulb exploded, leaving the hall-way in darkness. 'What the hell's going on?'

He shivered and rubbed his hands together. 'Crikey; it's cold round here.' He sighed to himself, wearily, and shook his head. 'Rigby was right. This was a damn fool idea.'

He walked, with careful tread, along the hallway, past the portrait of the Seventh Earl, then nearly tripped over something on the floor.

He stooped down and tried to discern what it was. Not able to see with any distinction in the frail and tenuous light, he stretched out his hands to feel the contours of that obstacle. It was a human body that lay, on the floor, before him. Through the sudden brilliance of a lightning flash he saw it was his companion, Rigby. There was no motion in the body. Not the sound of a breath. A second lightning flash revealed that Rigby's eyes were dilated, and his face contorted into a grimace of terror. He was obvi-ously dead.

Icy fear gripped his body. He looked across at the portrait of the Seventh Earl, then down at the corpse, as thunder roared without. It seemed that the story of the ghost was no mere tourist gimmick after all. There was some presence in the East Wing. And an awesome one at that, judging by the death contortions of his former companion.

'I've got to get out of here,' he told himself, as another detonation of lightning lit the hallway, then left it in darkness. He speedily made his way along the gloomy corridor, his hands trembling, sweat beading on his brow. The whole venture now seemed far from the light-hearted jape it was intended to be. And the idea of some fearful ghost of a long dead an-cestor emanating from the nether regions seemed a far from incredible prospect. And not one that he relished at all. He was determined to make it beyond the access door before any further nasty surprises were sprung upon him.

He ran down the steps, two and three at a time, in his urgency to fly from that detested wing. But halfway down the stairs, he stopped in his tracks. There was something, some shadowy entity, stood before the access door, as if to bar his path to the rest of the Manor. 'What the hell is it!' he asked himself, his voice shaking. Then a bolt of lightning answered his en-treaty. In the shaft of light the ghostly presence of a distinct individual be-came apparent to him. He wore a faded blue coat, a three cornered hat and boots with large, metal buckles. There was no question about it; it was the Seventh Earl that stood before him. Darkness fell, and the shadowy entity moved away from the door, with a heavy, measured tread, towards him. Hideous, mirthless laughter, emanated from its lips, as at some strange, perverse, enjoyment.

'No!' He shook his head in panic. Feeling nauseous with fear, he turned on his heels and ran up the stairway, back into the Wing he had des-perately sought escape from. He ran into his room, ransacked a drawer of a bureau to retrieve a torch, and then ran out into the hallway again.

He stood—ashen-faced and visibly quaking—between his dead com-panion and the portrait of the old Earl. He heard the steady, relentless steps of the approaching creature. There was no way back. In his terror and contrition he promised himself that he would never set foot in that Wing again. Even during the day-time hours.

The question however was how he would get out of it. Slowly, inex-orably, the figure approached. He switched on the torch and shone the cone of its light onto the approaching creature. The light revealed a cor-pulent form, a bloated and ravaged face, and veined eyes that were fixed on him, with some unfathomable and malign intent. He was even more ghastly and repellent than the unflattering illustration of him in the Reverend Foxglove's book. And there was a lingering smell of corruption about him. The dry, ghoulish chuckle was heard again, issuing from bloodless lips that were pulled into the most hideous, inhuman grimace, revealing worn and blackened teeth.

'Good of you to keep me company tonight, cousin,' he informed his terrified descendant. 'I feel we have so much in common with each oth-er.' The same heartless laughter followed.

'Get away from me you filthy creature!' he screamed at the hideous emanation. But the creature continued its steady advance. He stood, like a quivering jelly, and felt, with each new step his ancestor made towards him, his very sanity giving way. That same terrible fate that had befallen Rigby now seemed about to engulf him.

He ran back to the very end of the Wing. He tore open the curtains of a window, as the steps of his ancestor approached ever closer. A fork of lightning illuminated the trees, grass and hills that lay beyond the manor house. He cast aside his torch, picked up an antique stool and smashed the glass of the window out of its frame. With blind panic, as his ancestor shouted, and spluttered, and raised his arms, he jumped through the jagged opening of the window, cutting his hands and face in the process. Fortunately, some tree branches decelerated his fall; though his head struck a stone, and he was knocked out cold.

***

'My God, what's been going on here?' exclaimed Melchett, when he saw the body the next morning.

Manderville was taken to a nearby hospital. As soon as he emerged from his coma he was questioned by the police, concerning the bizarre death of his associate, Rigby. But what he had to say about the ghost of the Seventh Earl was greeted with much skepticism and the death of Rigby was put down to a seizure, with no suspicious circumstances involved.

He returned back to the Manor a few days later. He was an utterly changed man. A somber, taciturn and more introspective person altogether. And he was also haunted by guilt, at the terrible death of his companion, that was brought about through his own wilful arrogance. He gave up the booze and drugs; shaved and bathed regularly, had his hair cut to a reasonable length and dressed in a more sober and conventional manner, to the surprise and satisfaction of Bidewell and Melchett, but to the consternation of Elaine. He saw to it, as a debt of honour, that Rigby's widow was financially secure. She left for London, shortly after his funeral, and the following year she married a restaurateur who she had met at a party.

Elaine, who now found the Earl to be an insufferable bore—and so unlike the wayward and mercurial partner of old—also left, and went to London, taking the child with her. There she began a fresh relationship with a visiting American businessman. Within weeks she had moved, with her new beau, to America, and severed all contact with the Earl.

The Earl—who seemed entirely indifferent to the breakdown of that relationship, and indeed the absence of his son; as if they were all part of a past that was now strange and alien to him—started to read books on mysticism and comparative religion. And though he had previously regarded religion as little more than an organised confidence trick, he became a Catholic. A year after his unwelcome encounter with his ancestor he renounced all his worldly goods and titles, then joined a Trappist order in Southern France, where he stayed till the end of his days.

A distant cousin, that the last Earl hardly knew, became the sole inheritor of Murcombe Manor.

Ward 5C

Susan Temple

It's late evening as I arrive and walk into the dim, sterile room. Crisp, starched sheets cover the bed and are drawn taut at the corners. I place my overnight bag on the only other piece of furniture, a reclining chair, and sit on the bed, waiting. Closing my eyes, I try to suppress my worst nightmare. A lifeless deformed being floating in darkness. My baby.

'Just leave the card and gift there for any member of staff, and they'll get it when they come on shift.' A senior nurse's professional voice echoes off the stark corridor walls. It's a small town, and a glance at the ward board as I entered informed me there are just two of us in tonight. The light over the bed flickers. At least, I think it did. I'm so exhausted from the lack of sleep from this pregnancy.

A nurse walks in, she looks about 12. Her badge reads Mia Maddock.

'Now then, we've all your details from when you called in earlier; let's get you settled in for the night and I'll get your blood pressure and stats. We'll have a quick listen-in to baby too. Do you know how much blood you've lost since you phoned?'

'I'm not sure, I've maybe had to change three pads,' I say nervously. The nurse has had excellent training, as I can't read from her face whether she is worried or not by the information I just gave her. Blood is never good.

'We'll get some bloods from you.'

More blood. Great.

After settling myself into the hard bed, I must doze off because, when I wake again, she's clipped a wire to my finger and is about to wrap a cuff around my arm. She smiles.

'That's nice you brought a doll in for baby,' she nods to the reclining chair.

'I didn't. It's not mine. Did someone visit?' I'm alarmed to think someone has been in the room without me knowing. I've no family that would visit, they abandoned me years ago and Ray, the baby's father is working abroad. Maybe it was left from the last occupant and I missed it when I arrived. I don't like it. It's ugly. The doll looks off grey and its hair is matted in places. There is a rip on the lace on the doll's dress.

'No love, nobody's been in.' I stare at the doll, my eyes heavy with sleep.

The nurse finishes up, listening to the baby's heartbeat on a monitor and tells me it's nice and strong. I feel relieved and exhale. Only, I see my breath. As if it's a snowy day at the park, my breath spreads out across the room. Like sea fog it slowly disappears.

'Was my temperature alright?' I ask as the nurse leaves.

She turns, 'Yes, perfect. Why?'

'No reason.' How odd.

'Try get some sleep. I'll be back for observations in four hours.'

I feel the baby move and smile. The bleeding is worrying but the due date is soon and I'm surely in the best place. The bottom of the bed creaks. Looking down near my feet, I see a circular dent in the sheets, as if someone has been sitting there. I kick my legs to erase the nonsense from the bed and my delusional mind. Rain streams down the window making long streaks like icy fingernail scratches. The wind has grown stronger since I arrived and is forcing a branch outside to furiously tap on the window pane. My fatigue is so great; hopefully none of this will matter.

Suddenly I wake up in a cold sweat and push my upper body up and off the bed. The curtain around the bed is moving. Slowly, it ripples along the fabric. It does it again. My eyes follow it, left along the side of the bed, along the bottom and up the right side. Panicked, I look across to the window, but it is shut—no breeze, no draft. Looking back at the cloth, there's a dark figure behind it. My throat is dry as I try to call out. I shut my eyes and try to swallow, and push down the crippling fear which is rising up in me.

'Nurse? Doctor?' No reply. What does this person want? Its shape grows larger as it appears to walk towards the curtain. I shut my eyes. Drawing on all my courage, I reopen them and climb out of the bed, slowly. My toes touch the freezing floor and my legs start to shake as I creep across the tiled floor and wrap my fingers around the edge of the screen. I take one final look at the dark, mysterious hidden figure. Inhaling a huge breath, I draw back the curtain in one swift, fluid motion. My eyes search the space for something, anything.

It is empty.

Turning back to the bed, I lift the water jug and shakily pour myself a glass of water, downing it rapidly.

Maybe I was dreaming or even sleep walking. My mother used to sleepwalk. She would have a whole conversation and always be in a panic looking for something she'd lost.

I jump out my skin as my assistance buzzer suddenly goes off. Staring along the cable to the button lying on the other side of the bed, I freeze. The device taunts me. It lies untouched.

Nurse Maddock appears promptly.

'Everything alright in here?' She turns the alarm off.

'I didn't buzz,' I whisper.

'You sure, love? You're up and out of bed ... let me quickly do your stats to double-check we're okay.' She efficiently goes through her routine. 'Blood pressure is fine.' The rip of the Velcro scrapes through my ears. 'Temperature is a bit high. We can give you some paracetamol to lower it. Oh, and I'll change the pad you're on.'

I look at my bed and the previously pristine pad is saturated in my blood. 'I'll just go get another one.' Nurse Maddock turns to leave the room. 'Oh! There's a pile here already.'

On the chair behind where the shadowy figure had previously appeared, lay a pile of new pads and clean folded sheets.

'Perfect', continues nurse Maddock, taking one and replacing my scarlet-stained old one. 'We will weigh this one. If you continue at this rate, we may need to top you up with a blood transfusion. Good job you buzzed.'

'But I didn't ...', my words hang in the room as she leaves, and the door clicks behind her.

The paracetamol and tiredness take effect and I sleep for a few hours. When I finally stir, I'm shivering as if someone has ripped the covers off me. Not wanting to fully wake, I search blindly for the sheets around the bed until, without warning, a hand grabs mine. I jerk away, scared and panting. I screw up my face. I want everything to go back to normal and to forget the feeling, but my body cannot forget. I am frozen in place and can't breathe. *Pull it together,* I internally mutter. *What kind of mum will you be if you can't face your fears?*

The shock of feeling a hand on my belly springs my eyes open involuntarily. Looking at my round belly in the dim light, there is nothing there. I turn the side light on. Shadows in the room grow long and thin, but at least there are places of light. On the bottom of the bed is a box of medicine.

Was someone trying to medicate me? Like one of those nurses, you see on documentaries who kill patients or babies so cleverly that no one knows for years.

Is it a ghost or a spirit seeking revenge? Wanting to harm future mothers as it couldn't conceive in this life, or killed her own child and wants to repeat the deed. My mind races and I'm startled when nurse Maddock unexpectedly enters the room and disturbs my barrage of disturbing theories.

'Someone left this medication,' I say holding out the box to her. 'Or did you?'

'Not me, love. I've not been here since last I saw you and Denise, Nurse Millbank, is feeding a baby in room five, giving the mum a rest.' Nurse Maddock turns the box over in her hands. 'How odd. This is the exact steroid the doctor was on the phone talking about giving to you; strengthens the baby sometimes if it comes too early or there might be problems. Gives it a boost and a helping hand. I'll just double check how it's ended up out ...' She leaves muttering to herself.

Nurse Maddock returns later and sure enough I receive the painful steroid in my buttocks. I glance at my watch and realise it's four AM.

***

A miracle.

By seven AM I am holding my crying baby boy in my arms. The birth feels a frantic blur. Waters breaking, blood, drips, injections, contractions, instructions, tiredness ... so tired, so very weak. Lots of people were in the room, different coloured uniforms and scrubs. Moving fast. There were kind voices, commanding voices ... and a whisper. I distinctly remember a whisper right into my left ear.

Push now, dear.

And again, Clara.

It's all worth it in the end.

Rennie's got you.

With the pain and blood loss I faded in and out of consciousness. I remember thinking the baby had come, yet it hadn't. I babbled something about not letting the spirit take my baby, that it was mine. I could barely move my body by the end, but I could hear everything. Especially the ticking of the clock on the wall.

Tick, tick, tick, tick.

***

When baby Noah and I are finally cleared to leave the small hospital, I hover at the nurse's station, waiting to show my gratitude and to say farewell.

A nurse picks up the gift and card, which has been on the desk since I arrived.

'Wrong name! No Rennie. Honestly! Who should this be for?', she calls to the other staff.

'Is Nurse Rennie not on this ward?', I enquire as I stand rocking Noah in his pram.

'The only Rennie that ever worked here, sweetheart, was a hundred years ago, so very unlikely she'll pick this up!', she chuckles.

'Although ...' cooed another staff member nearby.

'Now, Stella, stop your stories!' the first nurse interjects.

'Although what?' I press her for more. Stella smiles, obviously relishing a good captive listener. 'Although, some patients say she is still here with us, on the ward in spirit. Would be a good one to have if true. They say she managed to save many babies with her intuition, and the ones that died she dressed and sang to as if they'd never passed. Poor soul really, never had any family of her own; she even got buried in the hospital grounds rather than the cemetery. Under the rose tree out front. Think the plaque is still there.'

A buzzer goes and the Stella heads off down the quiet corridor.

The radio which had previously been crackling out a radio presenter's voice with the news, instead begins serenading listeners to 'Highland Fairy Lullaby'.

> *Ho-van, ho-van gorry o go,*
> *Gorry o go, gorry o go;*
> *Ho-van, ho-van gorry o go,*
> *She lost her darling baby*

My contact lens blurs and is dry from the hospital heat. I touch it to correct its alignment with my eye and gaze up the corridor to where Stella has disappeared into a side room. A nurse in a dated uniform is up the far end, with her back turned to me, with a group of small, pale children following her. The two nearest hold her hands.

She's humming the radio lullaby and swaying barefoot as she walks away. They dissolve when they come to the ray of sunshine with dust fragments which stream through the corridor window.

Him

Jim Gilbert

Jim loved his garden.

Three months back, it would have been a different story altogether. It had been a state, with its lumps, dips and hollows and many different levels, he had been unable to walk its length without tripping or stumbling.

But now ...

Three months of serious hard work—coupled with a world-wide pandemic—and it was now complete.

Lockdown had been both a blessing and a curse, his garden had needed attention for some time—yes, he had planted some fruit trees, but it needed more work than he had time to do it. But now, being categorised in a vulnerable group due to his age (and slight weight gain), he had both the time and the money to 'get something done', especially since all of his trips away had been cancelled due to Covid-19.

Now, there were three separate patio areas. All block-paved, each block laid by his own hand. There was also a new, bigger shed, several planters, and a large privacy screen; it was a different space altogether. Eight tons of excess soil had been moved, each ton shovelled and barrowed by Jim from his back garden to the front, loaded into large dump bags and carried away.

Then there were four tonnes of aggregate, two tonnes of sharp sand —again, all barrowed from the front garden to the back by himself—as well as the hundreds of paving blocks, dozens of bags of cement and timber.

And now, it was beautiful.

Especially the raised patio. This was the main feature of the garden, complete with its two wooden arbours, one on each side of his well-established buddleia tree. The dark wood finish contrasted with the beautiful long white flowers. It was simply gorgeous—and easily his favourite part.

Yes, Jim loved his garden.

But he didn't love *Him*.

The 'Man'—or *Him*, as Jim had come to call him, had started to show up in his garden around two weeks ago. At least that was when Jim had first noticed the ghostly, strange figure sat on one of the arbours. It could have been longer, but so much had been happening over the weeks. With the lockdown taking so long, these days seemed to stretch into one another with no real break, same shit, different day as Jim had once read.

But one thing was certain, Jim didn't like the look of *Him*.

There was something, actually a few things now he thought on it, that were very odd about *Him*. *He* wasn't like other people.

For one, Jim could almost see through *Him*.

Jim got such a fright the first time *He* showed up.

In his 71 years on this Earth, this was without a doubt one of the strangest things he had ever seen. Probably one of the most unnerving too.

He had been at the back door just looking at the work he had done in his garden, cup of coffee in hand, the warm morning sun on his face. It was one of the days where Jim could relax as the job was almost complete. That was when he caught sight of *Him* just sitting on one of the arbours.

Jim almost dropped his coffee such was his shock. He called after the Man, but *He* either didn't hear Jim's shouts or chose to ignore him altogether.

Instead, the figure just stood up, slowly came down the two steps leading to the raised patio and walked down and around the side of the house. *He* didn't even acknowledge Jim being there.

He was a gaunt, thin chap.

'No meat on his bones,' Jim's long-deceased mother would have said.

The Man looked unusually tall, well over six feet, with arms and legs that were stick thin, *His* hands had long, bony fingers clasped together behind *His* back. *He* wore what looked like a black suit, with a white shirt and thin black tie. It looked to Jim like a funeral suit.

Probably the worst feature was *His* pale, bald head. And that face.

Well, there was no face to speak of, not really, and that was the troubling thing.

No eyes, no nose and no mouth.

It made *Him* look odd, kind of sinister.

Jim had spent a lifetime reading people's faces. Their expressions, how they looked and reacted. The eyes especially could give your first insights into how someone was as a person. Truth lies and deceit all showed in them. The windows to the soul.

But *Him*.

Nothing.

He had just been sat there as if waiting for something—or someone.

On it went, for the next few days, *He* would come at roughly the same time each morning, staying an hour or so, then leaving.

Jim had waited for the man to go round the corner of the house a couple of days earlier before following, he couldn't have been more than a couple of seconds behind *Him*, but when Jim looked along the side of the house ...

Nothing.

The tall gate remained firmly shut but nobody was there.

It was as if *He* had simply vanished.

Jim figured then that He must have been some kind of ghost. Some poor soul either passing through or ...

... well, lost.

Being both respectful and nervous, Jim had thought it best to keep his distance at first. Maybe, given a little time *He* would move on or at least figure out where *He* was meant to be.

But still *He* came.

Jim got it into his head that maybe he should talk to *Him*, that maybe by showing a bit of compassion—albeit nervous compassion, he could help in some way. Figuring he was the only one who could 'see' *Him*, then it stood to reason that *He* could maybe see Jim.

Jim decided that tomorrow would be the day he 'spoke' to *Him*.

So here he sat, fresh coffee in his hand, waiting. Jim had decided that he would come out to his garden a little earlier than usual, he was hoping he may see just where this chap came from. He sat himself on the arbour next to where *He* would sit, showing that he—Jim, was here, but not imposing too much on *His*—the 'ghost', or whatever he was, personal space.

Jim had been certain he was alone when he came up here. In the warm morning air, he liked the change of perspective this view gave him. Already butterflies and bees were humming and flitting around the flowers on his tree.

Six peacock butterflies flitting and jostling for position on the flowers of the buddleia, distracted Jim momentarily. As he watched one of them flutter to a lower branch, settle on the flower and start to drink its fill of the intoxicating nectar, he saw the faint outline of a pointed shoe in the adjacent arbour.

Jim glanced to his right, saw two long pale hands resting on two bony knees.

There but not there, Jim thought.

The morning sunshine seemed chilled now, even though it was much warmer just moments before.

What should he do? Should he speak to *Him?* Would *He* even hear him? His throat felt dry, and he could feel his heart quickening in his aged chest.

Come on now Jim, he cursed himself inwardly. *No time to be afraid. Just small talk, you never know, if* He *is lost, you may be able to help* Him *along.*

Sitting forward, Jim glanced at *Him,* taking in his form. The guy certainly seemed a lot more sinister up close and personal like this, so much so, Jim found resisting the urge to just take to his heels and run away from this ... thing extremely difficult.

So many thoughts jostled and shoved their way to the front of his mind, what should he do? Should he say anything, or should he just leave well enough alone?

But Jim just sat there, coffee cup nestled in his frail—slightly shaking hand. Truth be told, he was scared, very much so—and that pissed Jim off. After all, this was just a ghost, nothing more. What harm could it possibly do to him? As his dear departed Mother told him, it's only the living that will hurt you, not the dead.

What seemed like the longest time passed, during which awkward seconds stretched into equally awkward minutes.

In the end, Jim took the bull by the horns.

'Hello,' he said. Not much, but it was a start.

The figure sat in the next arbour either didn't hear his greeting or simply didn't acknowledge Jim's presence like before, but simply sat there staring at the ground in front of him.

Jim was about to speak again when *He* turned his head towards him, tilting it quizzically to one side.

What Jim could only describe as some weird Rorschach-style pattern seemed to surface on its face. Dark splotches simply moved and appeared where the usual features—eyes, nose, mouth, should have been. Jim was fascinated by this and felt that it made *Him* less sinister.

'What?' *He* replied.

Jim took a breath, 'I said hello.'

Jim could have sworn those blotches formed an almost pleasant smile.

'Hello,' it replied.

'I've seen you sat here for a while now,' Jim continued. 'I thought you may have been lost or something.'

The thing tossed its head back, emitting a strange sound which could have been mistaken for a scream instead of a laugh, and that Rorschach pattern formed a dark stain across its head that looked more like a cavernous maw than a mouth.

'Did I say something funny?' Jim asked.

'No, no,' *He* replied. 'Please, forgive me, just it has been so long since I have spoken to, well to anyone.'

Jim smiled. 'Given your current appearance, I would say that's understandable.'

'Yes, you could say that. My appearance is probably not as inviting as some people would like it to be.'

Jim nodded, 'I guess so. My name is Jim.'

'I'm pleased to make your acquaintance Jim, my name is ...'

The ghost suddenly fell silent, the blotches on his face seemed to freeze in what could be deemed as a puzzled expression.

'Are you alright?' Jim asked, almost immediately wanting to kick himself, the guy was a ghost, clearly not alright.

'My name ...' It replied. 'I can't remember what it is.'

'Don't worry about it,' Jim said. 'We don't need names to hold a conversation.'

The thing looked around at the garden. 'It's very nice,' *He* said eventually.

'Sorry?' Jim smiled.

'Your garden,' *It* replied. 'It's very nice. I like to sit here, in the sun. I find it ... calming.'

'Yes, I'm pretty pleased with it,' Jim answered. 'It's taken some hard work, but it's nice now. Do you remember where you are from?'

He shook his head, 'Nowhere and everywhere I think.'

'That doesn't make sense,' Jim started. 'Though I'm not surprised.'

'Things have gotten a little fuzzy lately,' the ghost replied. 'As if pieces of who and what used to be me are slipping, fading somehow.'

Jim found himself at a loss, what could he say to comfort a man who was no longer alive and was possibly unaware of it?

He looked up at Jim, those blotches swimming and moving across *His* face like living stains. 'Can I share something with you,' *He* asked.

'Yes, of course you can. What is it?'

'For all I admire this place,' *It* gestured around the garden with *Its* outstretched, scrawny arm. 'I cannot help but feel that I should be some-place else instead.'

'Yes,' Jim agreed. 'If I can be honest with you, I think you should be someplace else.'

He looked at Jim, 'Really? How do you know this?'

'Well, when someone passes away, they leave their bodies here and their soul, or essence if you like, goes on to another place.'

'Where is this place? If what you say is true, why am I still here?'

'I figure you're lost,' Jim answered.

'Lost?' The blotches merged and swam together. 'Does that mean I have to stay here forever?'

'I don't think so,' Jim could sense the ghost's mood changing. 'You need someone to show you the way to the place you need to be.'

'Does this place have a name?' *It* asked.

'I only know the name that I was taught as a child,' Jim answered. 'We call it Heaven.'

'Heaven? How will I find it? What does it look like? You said someone would be able to show me the way ...'

'Some say that psychics could help you, they are people who can see spirit. They would tell you to go towards the light, at least that's what I have been led to believe.'

'Go towards the light?' *It* repeated.

'Yes,' Jim smiled. 'So I've been told ...'

'I think I know where it is,' the ghost replied.

'Really?'

'Yes, when I go down there,' *He* pointed down between the houses. 'There is a gap beyond which is a bright light.'

'Then that may be it,' Jim smiled. 'That could be the way.'

'Are you sure? Because it makes me feel very nervous when I see it, so instead of going through the gap, I stop.'

'Then what happens?' Jim asked.

He said nothing. *He* simply raised both arms in a gesture as if to emphasise where *He* was sitting.

'You just wind up here again?'

He nodded.

Jim shook his head, 'I think you're supposed to go through the gap towards the light.'

'I can't,' *It* replied.

'Why not?'

'It scares me.'

'That's as maybe,' Jim smiled reassuringly. 'If my understanding of this is correct, I think if you don't go through the gap, you will stay here forever, like a kind of limbo.'

'A limbo?' The blotches on *Its* face seemed to draw together. 'How so?'

'Simple, you will continue to go down towards the gap, stop, then reappear here. This will never change until you go through the gap towards the light. You need to understand, the urge you mentioned earlier, that is what it is telling you to do. You will never be at peace until you go through.'

'But ...' *It* shook its head, looking down at its feet like a sullen child. 'I am scared.'

Jim wanted to rest his hand on the thing's shoulder but couldn't. *Its* torment and indecision seemed very real—almost palpable.

'I don't know what else to say,' Jim spoke. 'The choice to go through has to be made by you. Now I don't mind chatting and having a coffee every morning with you, now I know who, or what you are. But for you, it may get old very quick. My mother used to say when you're in a tough spot like this, you should just rip the plaster off, get the pain over with.'

'I know you're speaking the truth,' *It* replied. 'Perhaps I should do just that.'

Jim nodded.

'Would you mind walking down there with me?'

Jim smiled, 'Yeah, of course.'

He stood up, waiting for *Him* to follow suit. He couldn't believe his earlier misgivings had been so wrong. As far-fetched as this whole thing sounded, this was just a spirit that needed to move on, and if he could help, so be it.

He stood up alongside Jim, who had to crane his neck to look at *His* 'face', the two set off down towards the side of the house.

They had gone only a few steps down the path and Jim was aware that *He* had fallen behind.

'Are you ok?' Jim asked.

The thing nodded, 'I'm just a little nervous.'

'I bet once you go through it will all be fine,' Jim wanted to encourage *Him* to continue. 'I've heard all of your loved ones will be waiting for you.'

'Really?' *It* answered, still reluctant to move any further.

'Yes,' Jim smiled. 'All members of your family who have gone before you, grandparents, parents ...'

'There it is,' *He* said—an urgent, almost fearful tone in his voice.

Jim stopped and looked around him but could see nothing. 'Where?' he asked.

'It's there, just ahead of you. Can you not see it?'

Jim shook his head, 'No, I can't see anything. But then again,' he smiled and turned back to Him. 'I haven't passed yet.'

The Rorschach blotches in *His* face suddenly struck a chord of terror in Jim's mind, one that he would hear for all eternity as he realised that this ... abhorrent thing had lied to him.

As the Thing raised its scrawny, bony arm in the air, *It* spoke the final three words Jim would ever hear in this world.

'You have now!'

The scrawny arm shot forward hitting Jim squarely in the chest. There was a crazy sensation, falling and screaming–though not his own, not yet at least.

Jim fell backwards, the wind knocked out of him and as he fell, he became aware of others around him, like him, poor unsuspecting fools running and screaming at the world he had just been pushed from but colliding against some unseen glass wall.

Invisible, to everyone else but each other. Terrified and manic souls trapped by this heinous creature.

A limbo.

Jim glanced back and caught a final glimpse of *Him*, the living stains on that blotched face holding an unmistakable and self-satisfied grin, then *He* disappeared–as did Jim.

Forever.

***

Mary stood at the open door looking out into her new garden. She had moved in here only three weeks ago, a beautiful bungalow with an amazing garden which she loved so very much. It was much better than the sheltered accommodation she had moved from. Here she was her own boss, free to come and go as she pleased.

Her new home had obviously been cared for by the previous tenant, whomever it had been, they had taken great care of the place and the garden too.

There were fruit trees, flower beds and planters. All well-manicured and well established. This was a place she could see herself living out the last years of her life both happy and contented.

Yes, all things considered, Mary loved the garden.

But she didn't love *Him*.

Just Before the War in Ukraine

WR James

(Jingle Ends.)

'Straight after the news, we'll be asking have you ever experienced the supernatural? Seen a ghost? You or a friend maybe? Both of you perhaps? What was it like? Were you scared? Was it clanking chains and did it have its head held underneath its arm? Or was it something more innocuous? A dead friend or perhaps it was someone who looked like a devil and did devilish things? Anything. Let's have your ghostly and devilish experiences now. Phone Jimmy Vinegar on 04567819 or email me at vinegar@wbc.co.uk and let me know what spook spooked you. What devil bedevilled you? Don't forget to leave your number just in case we want to get you onto the show. Now, in the run-up to the news at one o'clock let's hear this one. Sounds appropriate.'

(Intro of song starts to play.)

'The Devil went down to Georgia *by The Charlie Daniels Band.*'

***

George looked around at the tables which were all widely spaced and had at least one occupant at each. 'Shit,' she said under her breath. She didn't want to go inside but neither did she want to share a table. Much too close to the *hoi polloi,* and you never knew what you might pick up. There was one table, at the far end of the decking. A very large table, capable of sitting six or even eight and it was occupied by a lone figure.

George eyed the individual. He looked odd. Not dribblingly retarded or anything like that but, odd. He was wearing a black velvet jacket over a yellow floral shirt. The shirt was open at the neck and he wore a cravat. George hadn't seen a cravat in years. She remembered her father had worn them in his youth, along with bell bottoms, she'd seen the photos. But in this day and age, really? How *gauche*. Not just the cravat but he wore a gold monocle with a long chain and, to top it all off, a fiddler's cap. All very odd. No, George thought, she'd go inside.

As George made this decision the stranger got up and walked towards the bar. Ah, on his way out, George thought. Or, if he wasn't she'd still take the table. The stranger disappeared inside and George made a beeline for the vacated space. As she settled herself, the stranger was back at her side. George hadn't seen him return from the bar. It was as if he'd just appeared out of nowhere. He looked at George and smiled. She didn't know what to say so she apologised.

'Oh, I'm sorry. I thought you'd left.' She didn't bother getting up. Nine-tenths of the law and all that.

The stranger bowed.

'Liv-ved,' the stranger said and waited expectantly.

'Sorry?' George apologised again and this time started to rise. After all, it was a genuine mistake so why the character should be livid?

'Liv-ved.' The stranger said again. 'Ell, eye, vee, ee, dee. Pronounced Liv-ved. My name.' The stranger bowed again. Most odd, George thought and wished he'd stop doing that bowing thing.

'I'll move,' George offered. 'I was only com—'

'Please join me,' the stranger invited George.

George did not want to join the stranger. That was the last thing George wanted to do.

'Please,' the stranger insisted and placed a bottle and two glasses on the table in front of her. 'A jolly good job I brought two glasses.'

'Yes,' George said and immediately regretted joining in the conversation. That was almost tantamount to beginning a relationship. George didn't like relationships, they always ended messily.

'Good,' the stranger said and sat down opposite George with his back to the other customers. 'We can have a leetle drink,' Mr Lived said with what seemed a certain amount of glee.

'Oh, I really ...' George didn't finish her objection. The stranger had poured two glasses of a green liquid.

'Oh,' George said.

'*Salut*,' the stranger responded and before George knew what she was doing she was drinking the green liquid. It ran down her throat and burned his oesophagus and then settled in her stomach giving a not unpleasant glow. As soon as George put her glass down Mr Lived filled it up again.

'We have a leetle drink and a talk,' Mr Lived said and George, unable to help herself, picked up the glass and had another drink. Oh my God, she thought. I only came in for a coffee.

***

(Outro of song on the radio.)

'Now have you seen a ghost? We have someone here who claims they have seen lots of ghosts in their time. I'm talking this afternoon to witchfinder granny, Jane Buttkiss. How you doing Janey?'

'Fine Jimmy. Just fine. How are you?'

'Now tell us, Janey, how did you get into ...'

***

The radio faded into the background buzz of the bar. George looked at Mr Lived. Mr Lived looked at George and smiled. Mr Lived? Was that his surname George wondered. Liv-ved. It could be his first name. Seemingly having read George's thoughts Mr Lived gave his full name.

'Lived Raskolnikov.' He offered George his hand.

'Oh,' George took the hand. 'George, George Butterworth,'

'Ah, The Banks of Green Willow?'

George looked non-plussed.

'I fear thy kisses?'

Hang on, George thought. This was all a bit creepy. A bit non-PC. Not that she was a Woke nutter but personal space was paramount and he had crossed the line. No way was she having kisses with an old git like him on the banks of any green willow.

'The musician,' Mr Lived explained.

George still didn't know what Mr Lived was talking about. And of course, it should be Mr Raskolnikov but George could not think of him as anyone else except Mr Lived. The name with two syllables. Mr Liv-ved.

'It doesn't matter,' Mr Lived said and picked up his glass and drank his drink down in one, as if saluting someone. George almost expected him to hurl the glass across the deck into some imaginary fireplace like they do in Russian films when toasting the Czar. Unaccountably George also drank her drink in one and crashed her glass down on the table as well. Again that delicious feeling of a warm hug caressed her innards.

Mr Lived sat upright in his chair smiling and staring at George. George didn't like that. She didn't know what to say to the man but couldn't let the silence hang. So, as with most people today, having nothing to say she said something.

'Are you Russian?' Then George wondered if that could be construed as rude or, even worse, making assumptions about someone's ethnicity. That was a hanging offence these days. She started to apologise for the third time. 'Oh, sorry ...'

'No, not Russian. I come from much farther down than there.'

'Oh,' George was mortified. 'Ukraine? What a terrible mistake to make. And with all the trouble going on.'

'Much lower than that,' he said and smiled.

George couldn't think of anywhere lower than Ukraine that would give someone an accent like Stalin. Why had she even started on this subject? She saw her glass had been filled again. In desperation, and to get away from ethnicities, she grabbed her glass and gulped the contents down in one go. Mr Lived kept on smiling. Again, the drink spread a warm balm throughout her body. George felt quite drunk.

'Georgina.' George said out of the blue. Mr Lived raised his eyebrows. 'My full name,' George explained. 'Georgina. But I prefer George.'

She preferred George as she felt it set her out from the crowd. Well, had set her out. But now, with all these bloody alphabet people changing their sex and names like there was no tomorrow, it was quite a worry. She worried that people thought she might be transitioning. Adapting her socket for a plug or something. Quite gross. So she had been considering changing her name to Georgie but wasn't sure. Anyway, for now, it was George but might change.

Mr Lived nodded. Or was it a bow?

George giggled. George burped and raised her hand to her mouth. 'Oh, I'm sorry.' Why was she always apologizing?

Mr Lived nodded again. Or was it a bow? Oh, how George wished he would stop doing that. George started to speak, although she had nothing to say, and instead of words another burp issued forth. Mr Lived did not seem to notice and George felt she may have gotten away with that one. As she worried the radio came to the fore.

***

'Ted Bendy from Warrington. Hello Ted.'

'Hi, Jimmy'.

'So, you don't believe in ghosts or other spooky apparitions?'

'I fink anyone who believes in that rubbish ought to be strung up. It's pathetic. It's like people who put the wrong fuel in their cars. They should be shot. I'd shoot them, Jimmy, I'd ...'

***

As quickly as it had come to the fore the radio subsided into the background again. George laughed.

'Ghosts eh?' She looked at Mr Lived. She felt unaccountably happy after three glasses of the miraculous green liquid that she had drunk. She felt like talking with her newfound acquaintance as a friend and confidant.

'Ghosts,' George laughed again and threw her head back. Mr Lived filled her glass.

'Oooh, strong stuff that.' George observed.

'Absinth.' Mr Lived said.

'What, the stuff that sent Van Gogh mad so he'd cut off his ear.' George laughed.

'Not quite. You can't get that now. Real Absinth. It's *ersatz* now. Not real. But they keep a special bottle for me.'

'Oh. Jolly nice of them.' George picked up her glass. 'Well, the way I'm feeling after drinking this stuff, this stuff that's not real.' She winked at Mr Lived. A most disturbing sight. 'I can't even feel my head. It's gone numb.'

'It will pass.'

'I hope it does.'

'It always does.'

It did seem a strange thing to say. But George didn't mind. She was having a rare old time now. All that business about foreigners was in the past. She felt like having a good chin wag with her new friend, for friend he was. Perhaps it was the drink? She never drank at lunchtime but what the hell?

'Ghosts? Devils and demons?' Mr Lived mused. George was wrong-footed and had to think why her newfound friend would say such a thing. Then she remembered it was on the radio and she had scoffed at it.

'Yeah. Tosh. Hogwash. All rubbish.'

'You don't believe in the supernatural?'

George laughed and looked into Mr Lived's eyes. 'Do you?'

Mr Lived smiled. He never seemed to laugh, he just smiled. Smiled as if he had a secret. A secret that George wasn't privy to.

'Well, it's all fanny, isn't it? Bullshit?' She liked talking like this. A bit Del Boy-like. It was chummy as if she was one of the boys. Two states that George had never experienced before. Chumminess and being one of the boys. If her partner could hear her now she'd have a fit. So what? George was enjoying herself. She normally looked down on male conversation. All about sex and football with not a smidgen of intellectualism. Oh, and all those stereotypes they revelled in. Hooters, knockers and totty that was up for it. Pathetic. She had her doubts that most men could even read. But today, it felt good to be one of the boys. Although, somewhat above them. She felt liberated.

'Yeah. If devils and ghosts exist you tell me?' She held up her index finger. 'One, why do they always only come out at night when hardly anyone can see them? Like aliens, they're another lot. Two,' George held a second finger up. 'Why can't they communicate like normal people? Get on the radio or TV. Maybe write a column in the *Guardian*? Why do they have to be so secretive and hard to pin down? Three,' George held up a third finger but she didn't have a three. However, it didn't matter as Mr Lived came to his rescue.

'Perhaps they don't want to be seen?'

'Nah. Devils, demons, ghosts, witches, warlocks and all that guff. It's all rubbish. It's just people who want some attention.'

'So, you've never seen a ghost?' Or a witch? Or a warlock? Or The Devil?

As Mr Lived went through the list of ghoulish manifestations his voice seemed to drag out each word. By the time he got to the last, there was such intent and meaning that George was a little taken aback. She was reluctant to make her assertion but, after another drink, she did anyway.

'No, because they don't exist.'

Mr Lived winced and then nodded, as if to himself.

'See, it's like God.'

George couldn't stop herself. She didn't know what had gotten into her. She never usually opened up like this, not even to her partner. And to a stranger? But he didn't seem like a stranger.

'It's the same. God doesn't exist. It was just a load of blokes who wanted power to keep the peasants, the women and most of the populace under the thumb. Tote that barge, lift that bale and be grateful lest you burn in hellfire for all eternity. That's why we don't believe anymore. We got wise.'

'Wise?'

'Yes. Got rid of God and the Devil and all those fairy tales. We got feminism.'

'So God is dead?'

'Too right he is. I mean, as if a man could have done all this?' She swept her hand around the table but intended it to indicate the world. 'Dead as a doornail. Along with the patriarchy and all the other feather-bedders.'

'And so is Satan?'

'Never existed. Besides, if there isn't any God then there can't be any Satan. Easy. That's logic.' George gave a self-satisfied nod.

Mr Lived nodded.

'See with feminism and stuff,' George continued. 'All that mumbo-jumbo got seen for what it was. Just the rich and the church, oh and men, keeping the power to themselves. That's one of the things feminism did. It showed it all up for what it was. Like the emperor's new clothes. Someone saw the king's willy and started to laugh.' She tapped the side of her nose in confidence. 'It was probably pretty small if truth be told.' George shrieked with laughter. She hadn't realised how clever she could be. Oh yes, what an intellect she had, her wit was devastating. Yes, she'd show this old fogey, what did he know?

'And you believe that?' Mr Lived asked.

George immediately felt unsure of herself. It was the way he asked the question, like an accusation. George didn't like it. It was sort of personal and she didn't get personal. No one got personal, it just wasn't done. You didn't get personal until you knew everything about one another. She'd nip this in the bud now. Then she saw her glass was full again. It was like a never-ending glass. It was never empty. She looked at the bottle, glowing green in the sunlight on the table. That looked full as well. The colour gleamed like the purest jade. All most odd.

'So, if God is dead?' Mr Lived talked as if he was talking to himself. 'And therefore Satan is also dead.' George would not have been surprised if Mr Lived had counted each point off on his fingers. 'How did they die?' This last question was not rhetorical and George realised it was directed at her. She didn't know what to say. Then she did know what to say. The answer popped into her head with no effort on her part whatsoever. She let a cheesy grin spread over her bloated visage and said, confidentially, leaning towards her companion and almost falling off his chair as she tapped her nose again to indicate a confidence.

'Because they never existed in the first place.'

She sat up and laughed. Shrieked. She was on fire. If only there were other people around to hear her.

Mr Lived smiled that same obsequious smile that hinted at some inner knowledge. It was smug and had started to annoy George.

'Some think he died because of his love for man.' Mr Lived said. 'Now they would probably replace that with his love for woman. But none of that is true.'

'That's right,' George said confidently. 'You can't die if you never existed. Logic.' Oh, why couldn't everyone be as clever as she was?

'I see,' Mr Lived said. 'So, if God never existed; coincidently and by implication Satan couldn't have existed either, then there's nothing to worry about. No Heaven, no Hell, nothing. And, in that case, everything is allowed and we can do whatever we want. No retribution. Lovely.'

Mr Lived sat back as if what he had said was proof in itself. An axiom. A maxim.

'That's right,' George said smugly.

'And you believe that?'

George couldn't have this. No way. She'd already said why it was all nonsense. Was this chap stupid? Besides, she didn't understand what he meant.

'Of course. It's all made up and if you don't believe me tell me this.' George was leaning forward again and pointing rather rudely at Mr Lived. She noticed that as she talked spittle flew from her mouth but she didn't care. Not a remnant of Mr Lived's question remained in her befuddled brain but she had to say something. Keep the initiative.

'Why don't anyone ever see these things except when there's no one about? When they're alone and away from everybody, eh? Tell me. Why?'

She had already made this point but as her companion seemed a little slow on the uptake? George was feeling a little worse for wear but she'd have this bastard. She'd make him admit that it was all rubbish. Ghosts and devils and all that crap.

Mr Lived brought his hands together beneath his goatee, closed his eyes and seemed to be meditating. George had him. He didn't have an answer. The Rusky, Slavey whatever he was didn't have an answer. George fell back into her chair. *Fait accompli*. Victory. Checkmate and good night Vienna.

'So if I could show you something, erm—unusual?' The pause emphasized the "unusual". He had that same maddening smile on his face like he knew everything and George knew nothing. George was at him like a rat up a drain pipe.

'Go on then. Show me.' George demanded.

Her words echoed and reverberated in the air. George hadn't noticed until now that the day seemed much advanced. There was no longer any sunshine and a chill wind blew that made George shiver. The other customers had left too. There was only George and Mr Lived. The cold breeze caressed George again and chilled her. What time was it anyway?

Mr Lived leaned forward and held her with his eyes.

'Now George, would you like a leetle bet?'

George knew she wouldn't like a "leetle" bet but she couldn't say no. She couldn't back down now. In more of a choke than an answer, George said,

'OK.'

Mr Lived smiled again. 'Good,' and sat back in his chair with his chin resting on his pointed fingers. Time seemed stilled, as if it was waiting for something. George didn't like this one bit. Who did this fellow think he was? If in doubt, attack.

'Well, if you think you've got some magical powers or you can conjure up ghosts or demons or something then go ahead,' George would show him. 'You've picked on the wrong one here.'

Mr Lived didn't say anything but kept his gaze on her as if weighing something up.

'So what's the bet?' George asked. She'd show him. Always call their bluff.

'You want to bet?' Mr Lived queried.

George hadn't, but now he said it she again couldn't back down.

'You said a leetle bet.' She imitated his speech in mockery. 'You said, not me mister. Cold feet?'

Mr Lived shrugged his shoulders.

'Have you something in mind?' He asked.

'Anything,' George said expansively.

'Anything?'

'You name it buster.'

'Anything?'

'Anything.'

'Then something of little consequence perhaps? A little something to make it interesting?'

'Anything, you choose.'

Mr Lived thought for a moment and then he smiled that obsequious smile of his as if an idea had been switched on with a flick of a switch.

'The spirit?'

Mr Lived opened his arms to George as if to embrace her. George couldn't hold his gaze. She looked away and saw the bottle on the table. Well, that wasn't too much. Sure, if she lost—which she wouldn't—she'd be happy to pay for the booze. Yeah, why not.

'You're on,' she said with conviction.

Mr Lived looked away from her and along the street. He nodded his head as if pointing something out. George turned her gaze to see what Mr Lived was indicating.

Coming down the street was a small rat. Well, a ratty-looking man anyway, dressed in jockey's colours, breaches and a colourful cap. At his side walked a large ginger cat. A very large cat. Six foot six inches of a large ginger cat. The ratty man and the cat stopped by the balustrade of the decked area and greeted Mr Lived. They did not greet him by name but the ratty man took off his cap and the cat made a bow.

'And where are you off to my fine fellows,' Mr Lived asked the unusual pair.

'We're off to Yalta.' The ratty man said.

'We haven't been back since that business in 1945.' The cat purred.

'We really thought we'd done it then.' The ratty man said.

'Armageddon on the cheap.' the cat purred.

'Quite so,' Mr Lived said.

'And then again in '62,' the ratty mad said with regret as if he had lost something.

'Oh yes, 'I really thought atomic bombs and the two I put in charge would have done the job for us.'

'Ah, Nikita,' the ratty man remembered.

'And don't forget Johnny,' the cat added.

'But Vladimir Vladimirovich will get the job done,' the ratty man said confidently. 'We'll make sure of that. Will you come with us?' He asked Mr Lived hopefully.

'Do, please.' The cat purred.

George could not believe her eyes. A ratty-looking man accompanied by a six-foot-six ginger cat? Impossible. There must have been more in that absinth that the rascal had told her. Perhaps it was real absinth? Perhaps her drink had been spiked? You heard about such things.

'I would like to,' Mr Lived answered the pair, 'but I can't. I have some business in Moscow,' Mr Lived pronounced the word Moscow as a combination of the words moss and cow. 'I have to see a man about a dog. A Hortaya Borzaya,'

'A nice breed,' the ratty man said. 'Ukranian.'

The cat just hissed.

'Don't worry. The dog will get whipped and Vladimir Vladimirovich will end what we started in Yalta and almost finished in Cuba. I would think by then everywhere will be too hot for any but the most committed sun worshippers. But I have a leetle business here yet.'

Mr Lived turned to George. 'Have I won my bet?'

George saw red and reached out for the cat to feel his fur and see if it was a costume. The cat stepped back and hissed,

'It's a trick. They're just friends of yours got up in fancy dress. They ain't no ghosts. I bet you do this all the time. Ghosts, no bloody fear. You lose.'

Mr Lived looked George in the eye.

'Oh no, I never lose.' He said. 'Well, maybe once,' he added as an afterthought. 'I never said I would show you any ghosts particularly, although, that could be arranged. Your bet was anything unusual.'

George was going to protest but Mr Lived raised his hand to quiet her.

'But, I can understand your scepticism. You people, nowadays are always sceptical. Other than for what you think you believe in of course. No scepticism there.'

George wasn't having this.

'Halloween costumes, you must think I'm ...'

Mr Lived raised his hand again to silence George. She wished he'd stop doing that.

'Perhaps this will seal the deal?'

Mr Lived took his head off his shoulders and placed it on the table. It made a popping sound as it came off like a cork from a bottle. As the headless torso sat in the chair the head on the table continued to talk.

'Will that suffice?'

George was speechless. More than speechless. George was terrified. She could only gurgle as she looked at the disembodied head.

'Good. Now, the wager.'

'I'll pay.' George managed to stutter. 'How much?'

'Oh, nothing of consequence. Nothing of any real value.'

Mr Lived's body leaned towards George as if the head was still attached. It raised its arm and, with its index finger, touched a space above the neck where his nose would have been had the head still been attached.

'I'll let you into a leetle secret.' Mr Lived's head said. 'To you, it doesn't even exist.'

George sat frozen in her chair refusing to believe what she was seeing. She looked at the two characters on the road. The little ratty man was scratching himself. The cat was preening himself, rubbing a paw over his face and flattening his ears. Each time he brought the paw to his mouth for a further lick his flattened ears would spring back to attention. George turned back to Mr Lived. The torso still sat in the chair and the head had that infuriating smirk on its face. However, now George realised that Mr Lived did perhaps know more than she did.

'No, let me see.' The head said. 'What was it I wanted from you George?'

George could not speak she just gurgled and shook her head to indicate that she did not know.

'I know it's corny,' the head said. 'But the only thing that interests me are souls. I mean, I have all the wealth I could ever want. My health. A fatal attraction to both sexes.' He winked, 'You see George, I could say I move with the times but I make the times. Non-binary, that's me. Anyway, yes I remember. We agreed on your spirit.'

He smiled and at that moment the radio filled the void between them. Jimmy Vinegar was signing off.

***

'Right, before we go to the news we've got just enough time to hear one more song. One of my favourites and just right for the ghostly item we started with.'

(Intro starts playing.)

'Werewolves of London *by Waren Zevon. Bye for now, see you again* soon.'

***

Mr Lived's head cocked an ear.

'Oh, I do like this song,' the head said to its two companions. They nodded in agreement. Mr Lived's head was singing along and paying particular attention to the lyrics. Both of his companions were doing a little quick step on the pavement. George couldn't believe her eyes or her ears. She was transfixed, the world had gone mad. When the third verse started Mr Lived's body raised a very hairy finger in the air.

'Yes, that's a good idea.'

His body placed the finger on George's lips and prized them apart, pushing its arm right up to the elbow into George's mouth. The head grimaced as the torso jerked its arm back out of George's body. It brought out George's lungs. George gasped and, as the gouts of blood poured forth, she fell back into her chair, mouth agape. Mr Lived's head looked at the flapping lungs and the associated viscera for a moment and then, after a nod to the torso, the torso reached across and deposited the lungs into George's lap. At the same time, a small ball of light exited from George's mouth and Mr Lived's torso plucked the object from the air with the bloodied hand and palmed it into the mouth of the disembodied head. It disappeared as a magician would swallow an egg. That same smile played upon the head's lips. The smile that George had hated so much. The torso then picked up the head and placed it back on its neck. The reconstituted Mr Lived shook his shoulders as if to settle things in place. Head and body made a sucking sound as they reconnected.

'That's better.' Mr Lived sighed.

He turned to his companions. The ratty-looking man and the cat bowed to Mr Lived.

'Still going to Yalta my fine fellows?'

They both nodded.

'Don't forget your sunscreen, Mr Lived said, it's going to get very hot in that neck of the woods I shouldn't wonder.'

He turned back to George.

'My, my—you do look pale.'

George didn't say anything.

'Almost as if you'd seen a ghost.' Mr Lived said and smiled his smile again. 'Or the Devil.'

Never Put Yourself Into Your Art!

Robin Kilmister

Martin entered the foyer of the manor, skimming over the posters discussing the art he was about to see. He wasn't exactly happy about driving fifty miles to a private showing in the middle of nowhere, but his publisher was paying him a lot of money to attend. *Maybe I'll be able to write some fluff piece that my editor won't cut in half like last time*, he thought to himself. To say that he was grateful for his employment would be a major overstatement, he knew it was the only job he could get as a *professional* art critic but he expected more from life. Not the usual thrill that everyone wants, hearing stuff like that used to drive him up the proverbial wall. He just wanted lots of money, fine art and possibly a nice young thing he could attach his arm to at parties. In short, Martin Benson was not a very nice man.

'Ah, yes!' A short lady with glasses said, pointing at him and approaching quickly. 'You must be Mr Benson?'

'Yes,' he half sighed.

'Well done for getting here on time, most of the other guests are late.' She seemed very excited, which only annoyed Martin further.

'Is there going to be a speech or something?' he replied. 'Before we *actually* get to see the exhibits properly, I mean?'

'Of course.' She seemed concerned at his lack of interest. Once more, he sighed.

***

While the late artist's brother gave a very long and heartfelt speech, Martin struggled to keep his head up. He overheard the brother's words about the artist using previous tragedy to create his sculptures; Martin zoned out after he started talking about his strict work ethic. *The last thing I want to know is how often that idiot Stephen locked himself in a room*, he thought to himself. His eyelids felt heavy but they suddenly parted by the eruption of clapping from the people sitting around him. He shook his head to wake himself, half-heartedly clapping his hands together. As everyone got up out of their seats he realised it was finally time to look at the sculptures.

As he entered the exhibit room of the manor house, he saw the others stare in awe of the artistry on display. Martin merely chuckled. He looked closely at an acrylic statue of a monkey climbing on a branch. The colours were bright with a cartoon-like aesthetic; Martin was never impressed by the artist's work. He always hated Stephen's style, colour-palette, materials and especially the man himself.

'They're even tackier than I remember ...' he mumbled to himself before letting out a small chuckle.

He looked out of a nearby window, finding more enjoyment in looking at the plain grassland outside. He noticed that the only object in view was a strangely placed stone well. He glanced back at the exhibits, his eye being caught by an enormous plastic statue of a bright red T-rex with small splashes of yellow and orange. He walked over to it. *How garish*! His brow was so well-furrowed that he thought it might never buff back into it's original shape. Many of the on-lookers were still and silent as they took in the pieces around them.

'Excuse me?' a young lady asked Martin.

'What? Oh, yes?' he responded.

'Are you—' She was clearly nervous, her words trailing off.

'I'm Martin,' he said sternly. 'Martin Benson.' He felt it important to clarify. 'You are?'

He observed her clothing. She was wearing an all black dress with a veil covering her face and dark hair. The absolute picture of a mourning widow; she even had a handkerchief in her palm. However, Martin was sure that Stephen had no spouse before he died. The only people invited were his remaining family (only one brother) and various *important* people in the art world.

'Annabelle,' She answered. 'I'm sorry it's just ... I've read your works.'

'Really?' He smiled, 'You've read my submissions for the *A.R.T. Monthly* magazine?' He presumed that she must have been the editor of the magazine which he had recently submitted various articles to.

'No, I read your work in *Da-Vinci's Secret Art.*'

His grimace was louder than words could have ever been. He hated writing that damned piece for a cheap *Da-Vinci* one-off magazine destined to be discarded in the back of newsagents. He swallowed his pride, raised his martini glass to his lips and took a rather large swig. He forced his fakest smile.

'Oh yes! That one.'

'I loved how you described him as putting himself in his own work.'

'Oh yes?' he said feeling distant, remembering when he wrote that *hacky* line. *What stupid phrase*, he thought.

'What do you think of these works?' she asked with a genuine interest.

'Bah!' he chuckled 'Works? I don't think I'd quite call Steve's *works* art.'

'Oh?' She seemed confused.

'It's all just colourful plastic, cheap acrylic and even cheaper paints!' He scoffed at himself 'They're so tacky!' He took another big swig. 'I don't know why he ever changed his style, not that it was any better before.'

'He changed his style?' she asked.

'Oh yes, many times. It was a shame that he settled on this tripe, he might have eventually become half-decent.'

He looked at Annabelle who didn't seem upset or surprised. He felt strange saying something that didn't offend someone else so he took another swig. He didn't think it was the alcohol talking but he suddenly felt the urge to continue the conversation and possibly impress this young lady. After all, he always did have a thing for those with dark hair.

'I went to university with him, you know?' He added.

'Oh really?' She seemed intrigued, a smile even crept onto her red lips. 'What was he like?'

'Oh, you know. As insufferable as the rest of the other so-called *artists*. We were in different years but we had a bit of a spat once.' He tried to sound as casual as possible.

'Spat?'

'Yes. We were both going after the same girl. Couldn't get over the fact that she chose me over him. Of course that didn't stop him trying to woo her constantly.' Something crossed his mind and his mood changed. 'Shame what happened to her, really.'

'What happened to her?' Annabelle was hooked.

'Well, she snuck out to meet with him one night. I understood it as her trying to get rid of the wazzock but he was *convinced* that they were going to have a love affair. When I caught wind of it, I ran to the train-yard.'

'Trainyard?'

'That's where they were meeting. It was an old yard that only had the odd train going through it, not very busy at all. However ...' He took another swig. 'She saw me coming towards her and she ran onto the tracks at just the wrong time ...'

'I'm so sorry ...' Annabelle didn't seem shocked but her expression did falter slightly.

'Don't be, I was thinking of ending things between us anyway.' He was unfazed.

'But she died?' A flash of anger spread across her features.

'Yeah, well.' He took another much-needed big swig. 'Happens to us all.'

Annabelle stared at him for a few seconds then turned on her heels and walked away. When Martin lowered his glass, he shook it, seeing it was empty. He looked up to where Annabelle was but she was nowhere in sight. *Not the first time*, he thought. He looked around for somewhere he could get another drink, a waiter perhaps? *Hell, I'd settle for a manservant or dogsbody right now.* His mind was rife with negativity and thirst. He spied the back of a waiter in a white shirt with a black apron, he clicked his fingers to get their attention. The waiter was motionless and silent, Martin clicked his fingers again.

'Yoo hoo! Hello?' he called out but the waiter still didn't move. Martin huffed and quickly strided towards the fellow. 'Don't ignore me! Do you know who I am—'

He froze as he touched the man's shoulder. It was hard but not in the way that a shoulder usually is. He walked around to the front to see that the waiter was a plastic statue. He couldn't help but laugh at his own stupidity. He heard a chuckle from a small group of ladies next to him. He closed his eyes and shook his head.

'If there's anything more humiliating than talking to a dummy, I don't know what it is—' He stopped his joke short when he opened his eyes and saw the ladies' faces. They too were plastic. He started looking frantically around, making sure that nobody saw him talking to a bunch of plastic dummies. He walked towards another group of onlookers he saw enter the room with him earlier. He attempted to introduce himself but they were also plastic models. *Am I going crazy? Where the hell is everyone?* He glanced around again to see everyone was standing still and had a plastic sheen. Even Stephen's brother who sat at the back of the room was a plastic model.

Martin ran into the middle of the room, trying not to hyperventilate. He was panicking and looked back towards the entrance.

'Maybe I'll get some—' he began mumbling to himself.

'Fresh Air?' said a very deep and familiar voice.

Martin froze. He slowly looked behind himself only to see exhibits and the large T-rex. He let out a sigh of relief, believing himself to have imagined the voice. The T-rex turned it's head quickly to Martin's direction.

'Hello pipsqueak!' it said with a booming voice.

'Wha—What the f—' Martin trembled. He tried stepping backwards, only to fall on his back.

The T-rex leaned its head closer to Martin who sat up weakly.

'St—Stephen?!' Martin was incredulous.

'Correct, you turbulent hack!' the T-rex let out a mighty laugh and roared.

'How?!' Martin screamed.

'You said it best. An artist *really can* put himself in his work.' A sick smile formed on it's face.

Martin scrambled back up to his feet and tried backing away only to bump into Annabelle. He turned to face her but she was plastic too. He screamed and pushed her over to the floor where the veil fell off. He recognised her face immediately.

'You ... You made her!' He looked back at the T-rex. 'You always were a petulant child, you still haven't forgiven me?!'

'She died because of you, you fool!' The creature was furious, 'She called you a heartless, abusive bastard!'

'That turbulent hussy!' Martin scoffed. The T-rex roared and took a step closer toward Martin who whimpered.

'I hope you don't have any last words!' It boomed.

Martin saw a nearby window and took a chance by jumping straight through it. He wasn't ever trained in how to land properly so he slashed himself badly as he slammed hard onto the floor outside. Using nothing but adrenaline, he forced himself to stand and run towards the stone well.

The T-rex and other plastic statues came to the window and watched him as he ran.

'Oh! You're right, I could never bring myself to take another life!' the T-rex shouted with more sarcasm than Martin thought was possible. Not that it mattered as Martin was running for his life. He slid on the grass, crawling behind the well to hide. He tried to catch his breath as he rested.

He didn't hear the soft thud of plastic on stone as a model of a large green humanoid fish-like creature crawled out of the well. It towered over the cowering critic and quickly grabbed both sides of his head.

'Fuck it!' it shouted in Stephen's voice. 'You deserve to die!'

Martin screamed repeatedly as the fish-man pulled him into the well. Suddenly everything was silent except for a small 'plop'.

Pretty Pieces

David Maguire

'YOU STILL WANT TO MEET?'

Smoke wafts across the monitor, the only visible light illuminating a bare arm resting on the desk, hand tapping a cigarette into an ashtray,

The sound of fingers clacking on a keyboard. Then a pause.

The chat box flashes up on the screen. One word: 'SURE.'

He leans back, taking a long, leisurely, drag.

On the screen, a new message: 'THE PARK I MENTIONED EARLIER?'

Grinds the cigarette into the tray. Lights another. Savours the hit. And types: 'OK.' Stabs ENTER. Immediately re-attacks the keyboard. Another missive fires across cyberspace. Seconds later it's on the screen:

'YOU DEFINITELY 6FT 4?'

Drums his fingers on the laptop.

The reply, instant.

'YEAH. WHY? YOU LIKE TALL'

Question mark. Exclamation mark. Semi colon. End bracket. 'L O L'

He clicks back,

'YOU COULD SAY THAT'

A pause, then as an afterthought—semi colon. End bracket. Send.

'WHAT DO YOU LOOK LIKE?' comes the reply.

'WHAT WOULD YOU LIKE ME TO LOOK LIKE?'

No response. He grins. He has a pretty good idea what the other guy's doing right about now.

Finally,

'HMMM ... MY FANTASY MAN LOL ... BLOND HAIR, BLUE EYES, MUSCU-LAR ... AM I CLOSE?'

Snorts in amusement, the corners of his mouth turning up. Types,

'SPOT ON'

Another drag, the corresponding text almost immediate.

'COOL. MY LUCKY NIGHT'

Exclamation mark. Colon, *double* end brackets.

'SHALL WE SAY 20 MINUTES?'

Nicotine-stained fingers suffocate the tab end into its dying embers.

'MAKE IT 30'

Dot dot dot

'IT'LL GIVE ME TIME TO PUT ON MY FACE'

A wink. Obligatory exclamation mark, exclamation mark.

'MAKING AN EFFORT? THAT'S NICE. SEE YOU THERE.'

Followed by an X.

He flicks off the monitor, plunging the room into darkness.

***

The neon light in the bathroom flickers into life, casting a blue glow like a morgue. He lights a cigarette, regarding his naked form in the mirror with dispassionate, albino eyes.

Bald, skin saggy, wrinkled and mottled—flabby almost, like it doesn't quite 'fit'. It's the appearance of an old man. A very old man. A very sick old man. A very tall, sick old man.

He sucks in, deep, letting the drug course through his body. Regards a row of small white plastic containers arranged quite precisely on a shelf above the sink.

A shrivelled finger teases across them, stopping. Unscrews one, taking out a pair of contact lenses. Tilts his head back. Inserts the first. The second. Blinks his blue eyes into place.

***

In the dark bedroom, the neon from the bathroom guides him naked across the wooden floor to a very large wardrobe. He stands before it apprehensively. Then pulls back the chrome handles on either side.

Cold, icy air immediately gushes out, wrapping itself round him like a cloak. He breathes it in, closing his eyes, the sensation better than any nicotine hit. As the cold mist settles, he opens his eyes, facing a wall of twelve horizontal drawers, six on either side. Without hesitation he grabs the handle of the third from the top, right column, and gently levers it out.

It's not a drawer. It's a hard deep plastic suitcase. He carries it across the darkness to the bed, laying it delicately down like a lover. Fingers caress the latch before CLICK—the first lock pops. And CLICK, the second.

He lifts back the lid deferentially.

It's packed with ice, lit inside by the same neon blue from the bathroom, making it twinkle like diamonds.

Gently, fingers push through the cold gems, thrusting deeper, hand disappearing almost to the wrist.

He slowly pulls out something long, thin and colourless. Lays it out on the bed. Pulls out another, identical. Placed side by side they look almost like trouser legs, eerily tinged blue by the light.

More strange items, different shapes and sizes, all pale, are unearthed, laid out like the findings in an archaeological dig.

Rummages deeper—then pulls it out, holding it up like a trophy.

It's the mask of a young man, the eye, nostril and mouth holes cut out.

He slams the suitcase shut, plunging the room back into black.

There is the sound of something ripping. Then a satisfied sigh.

***

Midnight, and heavy rain pummels the car as it pulls smoothly into the deserted park. It stops, lights off, engine killed. From the driver's side, a brief flicker of a flame as a match strikes, then a red pinprick glow.

The sound of footsteps crunching on gravel. A hand tries the passenger door. It opens.

The soaked guy nervously ducks his head in, regarding the occupant. The car's interior light reveals a good-looking man, late twenties, blond tousled hair, athletic toned build, piercing blue eyes. A winning smile, perfect teeth, cigarette held in perfectly manicured fingers.

Soaked Guy's eyes gleam. Jumps in.

'Jesus ... you weren't kidding. You *are* my fantasy man!'

'I like to make an effort.'

Soaked Guy slides his hand between the driver's thighs.

'So do I ...'

The driver gently removes his hand.

'Not here.'

He winks, squeezing Soaked Guy's leg playfully. Then starts the car.

***

'Brrr ... it's cold in here.'

A light flickers on, the same faint neon as before, revealing a non-descript room, barren of personal belongings and trinkets of identity. Just the large wardrobe, bed, and in the corner a desk, computer and chair.

'A man of simple means, eh? I can dig minimalist.'

Soaked Guy's hand grabs Driver's groin.

'As long as that's *all* that's minimal about you ...'

Soaked Guy kisses him. Driver lets him. He has to. Then he gently pulls away.

'I need to go to the bathroom. Get undressed.'

'You don't waste any time do you?'

He disappears, sliding the bathroom door behind him, while his visitor quickly removes his jacket, shirt, unbuttoning his jeans.

He's fully naked by the time the bathroom door reopens.

The bedroom's owner leans in the doorway, also naked, visible through the transparent plastic raincoat he now wears.

'You're a fetish guy? ... I can dig that.'

He saunters forward.

'Wait!'

Stops.

'I want to admire you first.'

From the bathroom, a grin stretches across his perfect, almost plastic face. He eyes the visitor up and down approvingly. Tall—6ft 4—dark curly hair, brown eyes, a slight beard, possibly thirteen, maybe fourteen stone in weight. Not athletic, but decent. Age? Possible early twenties.

'What's your name?'

'What would you like it to be?'

A chuckle.

'I'll give you that. Let's call you Jake.'

'Jake it is, then.'

'Hi Jake.'

'Hi.'

'Bye Jake.'

He pulls out a handgun and fires.

The dart hits Jake hard in the neck. In seconds Jake's expression changes from fear to horror to shock, before he topples to the hard wooden floor.

Except he's no longer on a hard wooden floor. He's on plastic sheeting.

The last thing he witnesses, although blurred, is his predator strolling towards him. With the biggest hunting knife he's ever seen.

***

Raincoat spattered red, he hunches over Jake—or at least what's left of him. Lifts the cigarette to his mouth, fingers sticky with blood.

There's the familiar sound of ripping.

***

It's dawn when the hooded man emerges, carrying two large refuse sacks, full, sagging, though he doesn't seem to struggle. He carries them to the bottom of the garden, to a bonfire already burning. Flings them on. Allows the flames to crackle round the new fuel before he heads back up the path, back towards the house. Takes a quick look at the rest of the properties on either side. Boarded up, abandoned. No one's gonna disturb him. No one ever does. Because there's nobody else here.

He disappears inside, reappearing moments later, carrying the flimsiest of bags. So light, he tosses it across the garden onto the fire.

He watches it morph in the heat. He pulls back his hood, allowing his dark curly hair to spill out. Opens his mouth, wide, stretching the lips back, making it more flexible. He does this two, three times. A spark of ash floats towards his face and he bats it away from his brown eyes.

The flimsy bag splits open. What looks like the mask of an old man spills out. It melts like plastic and disappears instantly, swallowed by the flames.

He takes out a cigarette, allows it to work its magic.

It's a good day. This skin is young, firm, a nice tight fit. It should last him a while. Before he has to start looking for others.

He regards the cigarette, marvelling at the smooth, flawless skin that holds it.

Takes another drag. Then turns, and strolls back towards the house.

One Big Treat

Matthew Tett

Hannah often begged her parents to read her just one more creepy tale. She loved the one about scratchy claws at the ink-blank window, and another story where a big moon-faced 'thing' appeared in the early morning gloom. She couldn't get enough. She loved being scrunched up under the duvet, head peeping out, wide-eyed. She, quite literally and quite often, held her breath, particularly if her dad was reading to her: he did the world's best sound effects, and his voice was perfection.

'Dinner! Quick, it'll get cold!' Hannah's mum always said the same thing, shouting up the stairs, although it *never* was cold. Piled-high bowls of stew steamed on the table. Huge, plated lasagnes bubbled with molten cheese. It always took Hannah an age to start on her dinner; the 'cooling' blows did little. But down the stairs she dutifully went, knowing that the sooner dinner was over, the sooner bedtime would arrive—and the sooner she'd be tucked up, ready for yet another scary journey into darkness.

She loved the desire to be scared. Her parents did little to change it—they loved it, too, said she had an 'insatiable appetite for being scared' and always seemed to be looking for the next scary tale. 'You'll have nightmares with this one,' her dad said. 'I'd keep the light on if I were you!' Apparently, this was his way of warning Hannah about what was coming next, as if each turn of a book's page was worse than the previous one. But it did little. All it did was make Hannah want more, until ...

... until the day she didn't.

Lots of children won't sleep unless there is a cutesy sheep nightlight glowing inanely in the corner, or a softly spoken story is playing on a CD. But Hannah relished being scared. She liked her dad to pretend there was a skeleton in her wardrobe, its bony fingers clutching the door, or a pungent-smelling monster lurking under her bed, all foul breath, grumbling and growling. She often pleaded with her dad to lurch around her bedroom cross-eyed, acting like some sort of *Frankenstein*. She adored anything beyond the realms of the safe confines of suburbia.

It was a balmy July evening, with birds singing their tiny hearts out in the garden. Hannah's parents had left the windows open—they said how the house was a 'hot box, stuffy' and how it was good to 'clear the air'. Curtains reminded Hannah of the sails on a boat, and they made a funny 'oof' sound in the summer breeze. Outside, the delicate glass bells on the windchime tinkled. Hannah's mum said 'they're a bit Amityville' which was meant to be scary, but Hannah thought she'd like it, not that she had seen the film her mum referred to. She knew her mum and dad liked nothing more than a snuggle on the sofa, lights out, watching some scary movie. If she had had the chance, she'd have joined them, glued, transfixed. But it was her parents' time, when they shared long, smelly cigarettes and kissed. Sometimes, Hannah sat on the stairs and sneakily peeked through the banisters, loving the alley chases, the blood-curdling screams, the hideous monsters on the screen.

But on this summer's evening, Hannah's parents had gone out—'a rare treat, just to the Simpsons' down the road, and there won't be any children there, so ...' they'd said. It was warm out and Hannah could hear fun happening all around the neighbourhood, plus she'd been left with a boxed pizza, chocolate pouches and sugary pop: all was good. 'We're just a hop and a skip away, sweets' her mum had said as they walked down the path, the sun still strong in the sky. Hannah felt grown up. Her cousin, Ben, was 13 and his parents made a big fuss about leaving him for an hour. But Hannah didn't mind, and she was younger.

She put the pizza in the oven, poured a bubbly glass of cola, and lined up her sweet treats on the lounge coffee table. She planned to devour the pizza, which would be covered in stringy, gooey cheese, and wash it down with greedy gulps of fizz, then move on to the chocolate buttons, the crunchy-shelled nuts. She loved how they shattered like glass between her teeth. Upstairs she went, buzzing at the thought of her dinner, but also pretending that something was hiding behind the airing cupboard door, that the creaking was not the day's heat affecting the floorboards, but that an old, crinkle-faced witch was stepping closer and closer, reaching out with her gnarled fingers ...

Hannah tiptoed around, loving the kick she got from the whole experience. Wafts of deliciousness came up the stairs. She wondered if she could watch something creepy—she thought she knew the passcode for the television. In her bedroom she patted her book of *Short Shockers*, grinned at the ghoul which was on her bookmark. She wished her dad was there to read her the one about the babysitter again—even though she knew what would happen, knew that the babysitter would have the fright of her life, she never tired of hearing it. The smell was getting stronger, and Hannah was hungry for the golden pizza, for everything that followed.

She went back down the stairs, humming and saying 'do-to-do-to-do' in as deep a voice as she could muster, all in rhythm with her deliberate clompy footsteps. Hannah swung her ponytail from side to side, made her way towards the kitchen, towards the heavenly aroma of pizza, and then her feast of chocolate, wanting to make the most of it as it was all one big treat.

Then, she saw it. It was a huge mass of black, something like a grotesque shadow. There it was, in the corner of the kitchen. The oven light was glowing. The bottle of pop stood open on the counter. She could smell it then, earthy, raw; it had taken over from the glorious pizza aroma, and now it was as if something hideous had arrived. This something was like all her favourite scary stories and tales had moulded into one great big thing, slouched there, stinking, in the kitchen, next to the family's noticeboard. She began to back away, to move towards the front door, or back up the stairs, when it looked up at her.

And this was when Hannah, aged 10, lover of all things scary, of monsters under the bed and ghosts clawing at the patio doors, wished that all of this was neatly packed away in her fantasies, and not sitting in her house on a hot July evening, when her parents were so near, but so far, at the Simpsons' house down the road. This was when she'd wished, just wished, things could go back to words on a page, to lurid drawings in a book.

It was too late, then, to wish for anything different. And as the creature moved towards Hannah, she remembered her dad always saying 'Be careful what you wish for. You never know, it just might come true.'

An Ill-Fated Journey

Kenneth Walker

The ships had started out in a caravan of five, traveling from the Colony of Brazil back to their homes in Portugal. Vento Favorecido, Aqua Lisa, Tesouro Dourado, Riqueza do Rei, and Má Sorte, All sailed regally in the caravan carrying loads of sugar and coffee back to Europe to sell to the nobility across the continent.

They had been on the water for five days and had just begun to reach where the warm waters of the Caribbean Sea began to mix with the cold, deeper waters of the Atlantic. Each ship was captained by a veteran of many voyages between Europe and the New World. On the Má Sorte, Captain João Antunes had been with Cabral when he had discovered Brazil. He soon was given his own ship to master. He had recently been given the Sorte as his own.

The trip to Brazil had been uneventful. They loaded their stores with coffee and sugar like the other ships in their caravan. João had not acquired a taste for the sweet, white, powdery sugar like many had. But he did make sure he had a personal store of the dark coffee beans whenever he was in Brazil. He ground his own beans and found the strong, dark brew helped with long nights on the ship watching for trouble along the waters.

He had never given much credence to the legends of monsters and great evil that was said to be 'at the edge of the world.' Instead he believed that he was destined to explore the unknown corners of the world. He had never seen a dragon or kraken in his travels. He would chuckle to himself whenever he heard young, inexperienced crew members talk about mermaids, either in fear or lust. His first mate, Dinis Montero, had been with João for five years now; he thought it apt that his name meant 'mountain', Dinis was the foundation that kept his ship running smoothly. If there was trouble with the crew, Dinis would handle it before it could be brought to his attention.

Another important member of his crew was his pilot, Leo Maia, Leo came from a distinguished merchant family that had profited from the trade between Europe and the New World. All of Leo's brothers were ether pilots or captains of their own ships in the family trading business. Leo had been taken on by João as a favour to his father. About a year ago, Leo had demonstrated an intuitive knowledge of ships and the water. He seemed to sense when the wind would change and had the ship ready to turn before it was needed. The rest of the crew was pretty much anonymous to him. Seemed like half the crew would change at each new port. Either replacing those that had died during the trip, or those that wanted to stay wherever they were and attempt a new life on land. They always seemed to be taking on new crew whenever they were about to leave.

As usual, the Captain was walking the ship before retiring for the night. He could tell that they were leaving the Caribbean behind and entering the wider ocean by the dropping temperatures at night. Without the warm tropical waters, the air chilled as the sky darkened. He walked back to check to see if the watch was staying awake at the back of the ship. Thinking he heard a splash in the water, he looked over the edge of the ship but didn't find anything. The watch stood quickly as he walked up. João wasn't surprised. He had heard Montero tell the story of how he had just simply dumped a sleeping watch over the edge of the boat, letting the water wake them up. The story was true. The part he didn't tell was that it was in port so the crew member was able to get back onto the ship before they left port. But, he was sure the story had Montero's intended effect and had them worried about being awakened by hitting cold ocean water. So night watches should be very attentive for the trip back to their homes in Portugal. He knew that some of the crew had asked permission to drag a net behind the boat to try to catch some fish to supplement their food store on the trip home. He had said yes, but hadn't asked how they did. As he returned to his cabin, he looked across the water. He was unable to see any of the other boats in the caravan. It wasn't a big concern, they were the last ship so the only place he could see one was ahead. It was dark so it wasn't unusual to not be able to see one of the other ships. So he went to his cabin, and went to bed.

The next morning, when Captain Antunes exited his cabin, Leo was at the wheel with a concerned look on his face. When the Captain asked him what was wrong, he told him that he had risen early and came to relieve the night pilot and he was gone. There had been no sign of him, the only signs that anyone had been there were several trails of water that led to the edge of the boat. The Captain scanned the horizon and found that he still couldn't see any of the other boats in the caravan. This concerned him now. Without knowing how long there hadn't been anyone at the wheel last night, he couldn't tell how far they may have drifted away from the others. He checked the sky and saw a storm was almost on them and that's when he realised they had greatly drifted off course, and back towards the Caribbean. They had already passed this storm and were drifting back towards it. He ordered the crew to lower the sails and cover every port on the ship to keep the hold from flooding from the rain. As he toured below decks insuring there were no leaks, the storm hit. He also looked for the missing crewman. He asked the cook, Tiago Pais, if he had seen the man and was told that he never came to get his morning meal. Captain Antunes asked several of the men if they had seen their missing crew-mate. No one had seen him, but some of them seemed guarded while talking to their Captain. He didn't think they were lying about the missing sailor. But there did seem to be something they were trying to hide from him.

When he got back up on the deck, Leo had himself prepared for the coming storm. He had lashed himself to the deck so neither wind nor wave would keep him from keeping the ship on its course. As the storm hit, the winds began to try to whip the ship around. One of the ship's crew remarked that it seemed as it Nature itself was angry with them. One of the young crewmen forgot to tie himself down, or go below decks and soon was washed over the side by a strong wave. The Captain got to the side as the man hit the water, there was nothing he could do. Anyone going into the water was just as likely to be lost themselves. The Captain sadly watched the young man sink into the deep. But at the end, the impossible seemed to happen, for just a moment, it seemed like there were hands pulling him underwater. João shook his head, and the image was gone. It would be two more days before they were able to escape the storm's wrath and in that time, he had lost four more sailors.

After the storm passed, Antunes and Montero checked the ship both above and below decks for damage. The sails luckily had been stored properly so they were ready to be raised when they caught the winds home. Below deck, other than the missing sailors, everything seemed to be in good shape as well. They noticed a barrel had been moved to the part of the ship where the sailors slept, but that wasn't unusual. The crew often used the barrels as tables for gambling on long voyages. He remarked to

Montero to remind them to put it back when they were done using it. He didn't need to waste a barrel of sugar or coffee if the crew destroyed it accidentally. As he checked the remaining crew, he noticed that all five of the men that had disappeared had been a part of the crew that had worked the nets for fish before the storm hit. He thought that was an unusual coincidence, but didn't see how it could have had anything to do with their absences. The day watch on the mast soon called out a land sighting. Captain Antunes scanned the horizon and found the island that had been sighted. It didn't look familiar to him, but it looked like it had a deep enough cove that they could pull in and he could have the crew check out the ship, and make sure there wasn't any damage to it. He directed Leo to sail for the island and place them within its cove. As they got closer, he noticed there was a coral reef that would make it more difficult to get into the cove. But once again, Leo's talents were up to the task and soon they were setting their anchor in the cove's sand.

The Captain separated the crew into three groups: one to go over the inside of the ship and see what supplies they might need from the island, one to go on shore and see what sources of fruit, meat and fresh water might be available, and one to go around the outside of the ship in the small shore boat to check for, and repair any damage they might find. Soon, it was just Captain Antunes on the deck of the ship. Montero had gone to supervise the group on shore, and Leo was supervising the repairs on the ship. He went below deck to check on the crew working down there and noticed that the barrel was still in the crew's quarters. He was about to move it himself when there came a scream from the water. He moved to the nearest porthole and found that some of the crew repairing the ship had fallen into the water, and disappeared. The screams hadn't come from the men that had fallen, but from their compatriots who had suddenly found them gone. Leo was trying to get them to calm down. They were sputtering nonsense about fish people grabbing their friends and coming for them next.

When he returned to the ship, Montero found the story amusing. Apparently they had found a small stone structure back into the trees. It had on its walls images of half human, half fish creatures. Montero commented that if there really were Mer-People then that's what they probably would look like. He said it showed people worshipping the Mer-People, and sacrificing others to them as a punishment for wrongdoing. The story seemed to unnerve some of the crew that had stayed on the ship. Regardless, Antunes decided to spend the night in the cove. Even though he would never admit it, the Captain knew that piloting the ship through the storm sapped the strength of his talented pilot, and he wanted to give him some rest. They took the shore boat to the beach, and some of the crew built a fire on the shore and spent the night there. The Captain decided to join them. He made sure he had both his flintlock pistols on him and had plenty of shot and powder for them in case some wild animal became attracted to their fire.

The two sailors who hadn't disappeared from the boat still appeared shaken by the experience. They were less anxious, but still insisted that someone or something had pulled their friends out of the boat and into the water. The fact that neither body had been found was not helping to convince them that they were wrong. So, they were more than happy to join those sleeping on shore that night. Captain Antunes and five crew built a fire and ate a meal from a small deer-like creature that they had found on the island. They sent some of the cooked meat back to those on the ship and kept the rest for themselves. As the men began to fall asleep, Antunes found it hard to find slumber, this was nothing new. He always slept better on his boat than on land. He got up to tend the fire when he saw what appeared to be someone walking up to their camp. He, at first, believed it to be one of his crew. But, a quick count showed all the men that had come ashore with him were asleep around the fire. He asked the figure to identify themselves.

He just heard 'Where is she?' in reply.

Again, he asked who were they. Thinking to himself that whatever crew member this was paying a trick on his fellow crew was going to be on night watch for the remainder of the trip.

Again the only reply heard was 'Where is she?' But, this time it came from all around him. He spun around and saw two of the shadowy figures right behind him. They grabbed him and he instantly realised these weren't members of his crew. Their hands were wet and rough, not unlike the skin of a fish. He then noticed that some of these beings were grabbing his crew and beginning to drag them to the water. He was able to get a hand free and pulled one of his flintlocks and shot one of the creatures holding him. It fell immediately. This allowed him to get free and shoot one of the other creatures trying to take his crew to the water. Again, all the creatures would say was 'Where is she?' Antunes ran to where the creature he had shot had dropped his crew member. It was Duarte Viana. He was a veteran of the seas and had sailed the ocean for years. He helped

Duarte up, almost dropping him as he looked at the creature that had cap-tured his crew. It had the upper body of a person, but the legs were gone. Instead there was the lower body of a fish. He couldn't believe his eyes, Mer-People were real. They were able to stumble to the shore boat and as they were about to push off from the shore, a shot rang out into the sky from the ship. That was the agreed upon warning that there was trouble on the ship. They launched into the cove. The call of 'Where is she?' followed them into the water.

On the ship, their hands were full with these creatures as well, Leo and Montero had been struggling to fight them back. Just as on shore, all they would say was 'Where is she?' They were able to keep them at bay on the ship with swords and clubs. But, every now and then one of the creatures would get past one of them and drag someone over the side or shred a crew member's body with its sharp claws. Soon it was just Montero, Leo and a crew member hiding under a bench. When the First Mate saw the cowardly crew hiding he told him to get up and fight for his life.

The sailor just responded, 'They're here for her.'

Montero gave his sword to Leo and turns to the submissive sailor. 'What do you mean, they're here for her?'

The sailor began to tell him how the night they had set the nets for fish behind the ship they had caught more than they realised. With the fish was a small three feet long creature with the upper body of a young girl and the lower body of a fish. The eight of them agreed to hide it and take it back to Europe and get rich, either showing it around to people or selling it to some rich noble. He was the only one left of the ones that had found it alive. Montero asked him where it was and he told them it was in the barrel in the crew quarters. They had filled the barrel with water to keep it alive.

It was about this time that the Captain and Duarte made it back to the ship. The attack had come to an impasse unexpectedly with only Leo defending against the Mer-People. They had backed up and stopped at-tacking. Montero quickly filled the Captain in on the sailor's story and then Duarte and the First Mate went and retrieved the barrel. The Captain opened the barrel and there was a small mermaid. He didn't know what else to call it. It appeared to be breathing, or at least if it was human it would be called breathing.

'Stop!' he called, 'Here she is, you can take her back.' Captain An-tunes backed away from the barrel and motioned his men to as well.

One of the creatures stepped forward, he looked more human than the others. He must have been older and more experienced in the trans-formation they go through.

'Why did you steal our young?' he asked in a near human voice.

'I believe it was just an accident,' the Captain replied. 'But, my men shouldn't have kept her captive. They should have returned her to the wa-ter.'

'Several were nearby. They saw her captured. She loved swimming with the fish. We believed it was safe since your ships rarely come through here.' The mer-man continued.

'Yes, we apologise for that, our leader in another ship wanted to try to find a faster path back to our homes. So we went through waters we normally don't,' Antunes said.

'We have punished all but one of those that imprisoned her. We must have the final monster for his punishment.'

Captain Antunes quickly realised they were referring to the sailor that was still hiding under the bench. Looking around his ship and seeing the bodies that had fallen across its deck, both Mer-People and human, Antunes just wanted the death to end.

'I understand your desire for retribution for the harm to your people,' he said. 'But I think there has been enough death for today. I give you my word that he will be punished for his actions here. I believe I can find something that will possibly make him wish he had been killed today. I pose that we strand him on the island. No supplies, maybe a sword to help build a shelter but no means to leave the island. And even if he does, your people will be waiting for him in the water.'

'That is acceptable,' the mer-man replied. 'If you agree to stay away from these waters, forever. If you come back we will attack again. I believe you will honour your word. You have already shown your ability to co-exist with those that are different.'

'I can only speak for myself, and my crew. But I will make sure this area is labeled as "proceed at your own risk". That should keep all but the most foolhardy of Captains from sailing though this area. We will also spread a description of the island so if it is seen they know to turn away from the area. Now, we will step back and let you retrieve you dead. Then after you leave we will do the same.'

The leader of the Mer-People came up to the barrel and pulled the child out. He handed the child to another who immediately dived over the side and returned it to their underwater home. He and the others then began to gather their fallen and returned to the deep, leaving five human survivors on the boat.

Captain Antunes and the other survivors prepared the remaining bodies for transport home. They wrapped them in cloth and carried them down below in the cargo area. Then they took the surviving kidnapper back to the island and left him with only the clothes on his back and a machete. They realised that it would be easier to get back to a known island in the Caribbean. So they sailed the ship out of the cove, took a star reading and headed west. As they sailed, the Captain found himself on the deck with Leo as he piloted the ship.

'I have a question for you, Leo?' he asked.

'Yes, Captain,' Leo answered.

'When I arrived at the ship, they stepped back when you were the only one armed. Do you know why?'

'No, sir,' Leo replied.

'He also seemed to be looking at you when he made his remark about me and those that are different. Do you know anything about that?'

'That I may sir. I am different from the other men on the ship,' Leo told him matter of factly.

'What do you mean different? How are you different from me?'

'Captain, I was born with a body different from my brothers.'

'Different how?'

'I was born missing body parts that other men have.'

'You're a girl?'

'No, sir. I was raised as a boy with my brothers. I am an adult now, so I am a man. My family recognises and accepts my differences. I am a son of the Maia Shipping Company.'

'Well,' Antunes paused. 'This is just the peak of discoveries on this day. I have never seen a finer boat pilot than you. And, I imagine you will be one of the finest captains the water has ever seen. Do you think they sensed your differences and that some how caught them off guard?'

'That's possible sir. I know you laugh off the stories of monsters and sea creatures. But I have always found them interesting. I once talked to one of my father's crew that had retired and taught young sailors how to sail. He said that he "talked" to a mermaid once and he believed that something about a man's smell attracted mermaids and drove mermen into a rage. He also told me that a dolphin will bring you a giant pearl if you gave it a fresh rose. So believe what you want.'

'Well whatever you believe in, I don't care about any differences you have in your body. You are the best pilot I have ever had and you aren't going anywhere until your family drags you back to the family shipping company,' Antunes said.

Standing there watching the sky, Antunes decided that he still didn't believe in legends and superstitions. But, maybe a name change was in store for the ship. After this story'd get out, no one would want to sail on a ship called the *Ill Fate*.

The ship pulled away and no one looked back at the island. But if they had, they would have seen a figure hanging from a tree by a rope woven out of tree bark. The machete left behind stuck in the sand below him. They would have also seen a pair of figures emerge from the water and walk to where the man was hanging. They would have appeared to be an adult male and a young girl. They stood quietly and watched the man hang there. The male opened his hand and blew a powdery substance on the body. It started to smooth out, like the decay normally associated with death was being stopped. It also stiffened as if paralysed. The only thing that could move were his eyes. Almost like his body had become a living prison. The two of them stood there for a few seconds, then turned and returned to the water without saying a word.

Lurking Behind

Ivan Richardson

A floorboard creaked below the old carpet. Quiet enough to be hidden by the fan on Darren's laptop. But he still heard it. It was back again. A tap against the window. It was there, lurking behind him. Maybe three metres away on the other side of the room. Had it ever left? Darren carried on typing at his desk. Too much to do. Can't be distracted. With the sun long departed the white of his screen gave a small offering of light. A small desk side lamp struggled to make up the difference. Didn't matter. As long as he could see the text in front of him.

Something moved on the shelves near the window. A book maybe. What was it doing now? He turned around to an empty room. An old book was turned at a slight angle but sitting peacefully. It was gone. It always fled just as he turned to look. Where did it go?

Back to the laptop. Work to do. Another creak. Now in the middle of the room. Was it back already? Didn't matter. It shouldn't matter. The floor creaked again, even closer. The breeze of something moving tickled the hair on the back of his head. No point focusing on it. No point turning again. He just needed to carry on working.

'Hey babe.' Hannah came through the door holding a mug of hot chocolate. 'You working late again?' A baggy red t-shirt, once his, stretched almost to her knees.

'I've got too many reports to sort.'

'Do you? Come on, I'm sure they can wait till morning.'

'There's too much. Just one more. Then I'll join you.'

'It's not your problem if work doesn't hire enough staff.' She gave a repeated sigh. 'You're going to burn yourself out.'

'It's fine. I just need to get it done.'

The corners of her mouth dropped as she gazed over his shoulder. Could she see it behind him? It creaked again, it was there. If he asked, would she tell him what it looked like?

She took a sip of hot chocolate. Hands clasped around the mug. Was she trying to mask her fear?

'Is everything ok?' she asked. Eyes back on him.

'I'm fine,' he said. He wasn't the one to worry about. He wasn't the one who could see it. Why wasn't she running? 'I just need ...' There was no point explaining.

'I'll see you upstairs.' Her gaze returned to the space behind him as she backed out the room, clutching her mug. Flashes of fear shot across her face. Once out the study door she hurried up the stairs. He carried on typing to the sound of her brushing her teeth upstairs. The bedroom door opened. He closed his eyes for a moment as he imagined Hannah removing that t-shirt before climbing naked into bed. He remained at the desk. No time for distraction.

His mouth was dry. His water bottle was empty. He tried to push through but the scratching at the back of his throat was becoming a distraction. Cold kitchen tiles pressed through his socks as approached the sink. His hand felt along the wall. Fingertips passing over the plastic light switch, but he didn't use it. What if he saw its reflection in the kitchen window as it followed behind him. Better to stay in the dark. Hannah was already snoring upstairs. Something tapped against the kitchen cabinet. He didn't turn around. Eyes down as he turned the tap. Ice cold water spilled onto his aching hands.

A scratch against the kitchen tiles. Could he call out to it? Ask what it was, what it wanted. His lips parted but found no breath to call.

Bottle full, he closed his eyes before turning back to the study. Holding his breath before opening them again. The hallway was empty again. Only the silhouette of a side table painted in moonlight. Nothing between him and his work.

Tired eyes struggled to keep focus as he typed away. Just one more report. Then he could sleep. Something tapped on the window. He began writing more quickly, hoping the key strokes would drown all other noise. A book moved. Another book moved. He kept typing. Sentence after sentence. Word after word. On and on. Had to get it finished by morning.

If he could just get it done he could go upstairs. Finally he could lie next to Hannah for an hour or two. Feel her soft skin pressed against his own. Let his breath synchronise with hers as he rested. A thud from the centre of the room as if a foot slammed down a metre from Darren's chair. He remained focused. A louder thud, cracking the wooden floorboards in anger as he denied it attention.

Not now. Not when he was so close to finishing.

Re-reading what he'd written, he found constant mistakes and missing sections. That was no good. He needed to fix it. Fix all of it. Each time he read it there were more mistakes than before. With each keystroke the end grew further away. From behind him came the low rumble of air being inhaled and exhaled. Just behind the back of his head. Tickling the hairs on his neck.

Finally he finished the report. Hitting send on the email, it was no longer his concern. He stared up at the ceiling as aching fingers withdrew from the keyboard. The breaths behind him ceased. All he could hear was Hannah snoring above.

Silence was broken by the ping of incoming mail. More work. More writing. The breathing behind him grew to a growl. It rumbled from the back of some monstrous throat. Demanding respect.

He couldn't take it anymore. His lips parted. He filled his lungs ready to push the words out. 'Are you there?' His lips sealed as if to pull the words back again. His hands froze. Everything froze. The growl behind him boiled away leaving nothing but a mocking silence.

'Are you still there?' He raised his voice in desperation. Body still paralysed.

There was a long exhale, inches from Darren's head. A deep voice uttered a singled word. 'Yes.'

An Unoccupied House

Barlow Crassmont

'He comes out at the Skalding Manor, when the moon is full, and the wind howls in pain,' Osvaldo said. His eyes looked towards the nose, giving him an appearance of a medieval dungeon wacko. 'He doesn't walk, but glides, like on a skateboard. And you can see right through him.'

'Really? So he's made of ... smoke?'

Osvaldo shrugged, then added: '*Maybe.*'

'Does he say anything?' I asked. He leaned in, and briefly paused before replying.

'No, but he probably will soon. Tomorrow night, I'll ask him his name. You should come with me.'

He always whispered his theories while looking over both shoulders, like they were universal truths unfit for the curious bystander. Yet there was little chance of an eavesdropper. Osvaldo's poor hygiene ensured that most kept their distance, as if he was an open septic tank. My chronic anosmia made smelling an impossibility, so I was the rare friend who tolerated his foolish remarks from up close. Bullies like Robbie Miles, however, laughed behind his back, calling him 'a kook from Riverbrook', 'a dingbat with a shit-stained hat', and 'a mongrel of a drifter and Isla McConnell', seldom hesitating to show their cruelty to the poor boy. Two months ago, Robbie tripped Osvaldo in the cafeteria as he carried a loaded tray. The fall caused an uproar of laughter among the school's students. It also broke his jaw, which he's yet to fully recover from.

Still, there was some speculation in his beliefs that kept me from joining the masses in their abandonment of him.

'What time are you going?' I asked.

'He never appears before midnight.'

'My parents will never let me out that late!'

'That's what bedroom windows are for.' He winked.

And that was that. The instantaneous opening-and-closing of his right eye was the finalisation of an agreement that I would join him in his quest. We didn't shake on it, and we didn't have to. He knew I would keep my word, just as he was sure to prove he wasn't crazy to at least one person.

***

If not for the few scattered stars in the background that separated Skalding Manor's silhouette against the gloomy night, the house would otherwise be inseparable from the surrounding darkness. Even the silvery moon, upon laying its light briefly on the spooky property, soon lost interest in its appearance, and hid behind the passing clouds, never to appear again.

When Osvaldo and I approached the house in the ominous silence, the overgrown grass surrounding it swayed melodiously to and fro, as if waltzing to a muted version of the *Totentanz*.

'Come on,' Osvaldo whispered. 'He should be appearing soon.' The front porch creaked under our footsteps, and this squealing continued with the opening of the front door and our entering the house.

My only guide inside the dark interior was the back of Osvaldo's shirt, which I held on as if for dear life. I saw nothing but pure blackness in all directions.

'There he is!' Osvaldo exclaimed. I didn't know what he was looking at, nor in which direction. 'Do you see him?'

'I can't see anything,' I said.

'He's right there, clear as day!' His voice then spoke away from me. 'What is your name, boy?'

'It's too dark ...' I said. 'I don't ... I can't see *anything*.'

'You don't believe me.' Osvaldo's voice was breaking. 'No one does. They think I'm crazy.' The thick darkness could not shield my ears from his sobs, which soon morphed into a downpour of tears.

'Oz ... I'm sorry ... but I can't lie to you.'

'Why not?' His sniffles echoed in the vast space like reverberations of loneliness itself. 'Can't you at least pretend?'

His request landed with a thud on my heretofore subconsciousness. I realised what Osvaldo wanted above all else: a friend who not only accepted his lunacy, but one who played mad and joined him in his self-manufactured absurdity. My hand on his shoulder comforted him to some degree, but it was a mere precursor for my next move.

'Oh,' I whispered. 'I see him now. There ...' My voice resonated back at me, like a false response from night itself.

'Where?' he asked. 'Go on, show it to me.' I let go of his shirt, and ventured blindly ahead, until I could no longer tell if he was behind me, to my left, or to my right. 'Describe him to me.'

'He's ... he's pale,' I said. 'About 10 or 12 years old. His clothes are ragged, and quite dirty ...' The longer I spoke, the more I believed the fabrications I was spewing. At length, multiple giggles interrupted my thoughts, and my speech. The above lights suddenly came on, like a flash of lightning stretched to permanence, illuminating the ruined interior. On the stairway above me stood three boys, among which were Robbie Miles, Kevin Lockwood, and Mitch Finkle. And, much to my surprise, Osvaldo as well. Robbie held a night vision camera. The red light indicated it was still recording.

'Well, well,' Robbie said. 'What a fucking nut we have here.'

'What are you doing?' I asked. My disorientation was acute and overwhelming; for the moment, it appeared as if the room was spinning.

'The Kook from Riverbrook has a worthy match now.'

'You promised not to call me that anymore,' Osvaldo said. Robbie hesitated, then nodded reluctantly. He lowered his camera.

'When this shit goes viral, you'll be an international joke,' he said to me.

'What *is* this?' I glanced at Osvaldo, whose cunning smile was an unfamiliar expression on his aloof face. 'Osvaldo?' I willed him to respond with my stare, which he eventually did.

'It's the only way they'd stop making fun of me,' Osvaldo said. 'Now *you'll* be the idiot who talks about ghosts, and I'll be joining their gang.'

'We'll see about that,' Robbie snickered. 'You'll have to take a shower first.' His two companions giggled, like treacherous hyenas.

'The McConnell Mongrel thinks he's hot shit already,' cried Kevin, clapping joyfully. Mitch high-fived him. This infuriated Osvaldo.

'Robbie! You promised to make them stop calling me names if I brought him here!' His finger was pointed at me, and it stung like an Asian giant hornet.

Their laughter resonated like an avalanche of cacophony that ached the ears as much as the eyes, for its emission contorted their faces into expressions mischievous and perverse. Osvaldo avoided my prolonged gaze, and pretended to laugh with them only for the promised solidarity. I could sense he was devastated under the present mien of unified bullying, and fought hard to keep tears at bay.

But a sinister growl soon muted their display of hilarity, like a volume suddenly turned down. The sound originated upstairs, gradually making its way down the curvy stairwell, until the elongated howl flooded the room with its merciless vigour. The four boys screamed, their hands held over their aching ears, resembling ineffective patches against expanding holes on a sinking ship. I joined them in their panic, shutting my eyes and praying for the agony to end.

The torment lasted for an eternity, if it lasted a second. By the time it was over, the ensuing silence was equally deafening to my ringing ears. I kept my eyes closed, terrified of what I might see upon opening them. But the turbulent sound of external wind assured me the roaring force had now ventured outside. With shivering limbs, I gradually peeked at the remains of the departed spectacle. The room was eerily quiet, reminiscent of the sinister silence from before; the darkness prevalent and vast still. If anyone else was still in the vicinity, I could not tell, not even if they were in front of my face.

'H-hello ...?' My voice trembled, and only then did I realise that I had wet my pants unaware. The stench of my urine struck my nostrils like spoiled vinegar; for the first time in years, my smell had returned. I spoke several more times, called Osvaldo and Robbie's names, but my words went unanswered. At length, I extended my arms in front of me, and slowly felt my way around the adjacent walls, until I reached the main door. The outside was slightly more illuminated, and I staggered and fell on the tall, unkempt grass, after only a few steps. I wanted to cry, to discharge the fear and disappointment and the disgust that simmered in my belly, like a bubbling cauldron.

But no tears came, and the previous apprehension had dissipated, like the enchanted mist I now saw hovering near and far above the swaying grass. Some distance away, at the footsteps of the house, a hazy figure rose from the fog, as if exhaled from its excess. It resembled the stature of a boy, a pale one, or so it seemed from where I stood. Lingering about atop of the mist, it meandered its way toward me, its form growing larger. I could hardly believe my eyes, and my heart beat with the fervour of an antiquated alarm clock gone haywire. As my breath shortened, I struggled to breathe. My lightheadedness caused me to see two headlights breaking through the apparition, just before I fainted.

***

A bulky officer stood mere inches from my face when I woke up at the police station. He smelled of cigarettes and old man perspiration, and awkwardly adjusted his comb-over as I rubbed my groggy eyes.

'Can you tell me your name, boy?' he asked in a husky voice.

'J—,' I told him.

'What were you doing at Skalding Manor in the middle of the night?'

Should I lie or tell the truth? One option led to obstruction of justice, while the second labeled me a madman. 'My friend and I ... we went exploring.'

'You should know better than to go poking your nose in that place. Where is your friend?'

I shrugged. 'He ... left.' That was no lie, at least. No one was there when I left.

'Well, I should take you home. Your parents must be worried sick. Where do you live?'

'Sir,' I said. 'Did you see anyone at the house?'

He shook his head. 'It never occurred to me to go in there. You and your friends would be wise to do the same.'

***

I never saw Osvaldo again. The ensuing investigation proved fruitless, and at length, his disappearance, and that of the three boys, remained unsolved. Yet the citizens whispered and gossiped about their fate, especially their classmates. Those crazy enough to defy all warnings ventured to the outskirts of the cursed property at the gloomiest of hours still. Most claim not to have seen or heard a peep, even upon exploring the house's darkest cellars and basements.

But the select few, the social outcasts and victims of occasional peer bullying, swear to have caught a glimpse of a small enigmatic figure just before the appearance of the morning sun. They claim it stared at them from afar, luring them into the house with its inviting arm. It resembled a boy they once knew, one whose foul odour followed him even into the great beyond, but whose name they've long since forgotten, just like the foreboding reputation of the unoccupied house.

An Oldie, But Not a Goodie

Callum Melvein

Dear reader, beware the powers of the unknown. Hear these words of Stephen King, who once said 'Monsters are real, and ghosts are real too. They live inside us, and sometimes, they win.'

***

One hot, sunny day in Potosi, Missouri, on the twelfth of May 2010, there was a large group of people celebrating a little boy's birthday. The celebration took place in a park. It was a beautiful place with a big oak tree sitting in the centre of the park. Its leaves were full and thick, and the grass moved gently in the wind. Everything was wonderful; there were a lot of kids playing, parents chatting, and presents on the table.

But then, one of the mothers saw a lonely little girl sitting on a bench all alone. The woman went over to her and asked her gently, 'Hello, are you alright? Are you lost?' But the girl just remained silent, so the woman brought her inside her small white house near the park while everyone was playing outside.

She asked the little girl what her name was.

The girl said, 'Linda Edwards.'

Then the woman said, 'Don't worry; I'm going to find your parents.'

Five minutes later, there was the sound of a gunshot inside the house. So, one of the other parents went inside and found the body of the woman on the floor, shot in the back of the head, and Linda just sitting there, staring at the body.

Later, at the police station, Linda gave a statement about the incident and told them that an old man and woman committed the murder. Then her dad came to pick her up. He told them that he and Linda were shopping this morning, and she just disappeared when he turned his back for a minute. The police showed him the sketches of the man and woman his daughter described and asked if he knew them, but he said he didn't.

The next day, the police told the father they had identified the old couple as Ray and Faye Copeland, a serial killer couple from Arkansas in the 1980s. But the odd thing is they had been dead for years, so they wondered how they could have killed that woman if they were dead?

When the detective went to the house, he found Linda wandering the road. So he stopped and asked her, 'Linda, why are you out here?'

Then Linda said, 'There is someone behind you.' He turned around, and there was another gunshot.

Linda's father found her an hour later and discovered the detective's body. So he took Linda to a church to speak to his brother, the priest.

The priest said to him, 'Do you have anything to say, brother?'

He said, 'Yes, a year ago, I moved me and Linda to an old farm to get a fresh start. But then she began to act strange, talking to people who weren't there and remembering things that never happened to her. I learned that the farm was once owned by a couple, Ray and Faye Copeland, a husband and wife pair of serial killers who conned and murdered drifters. They died years ago, but I think my daughter has been possessed by them, and now people are dying around her. What do we do?'

The priest said, 'We must perform an exorcism on Linda; that might stop the Copelands.'

As the exorcism ritual began, the house trembled with supernatural fury. Objects levitated, paintings rattled on the walls, and unearthly voices reverberated throughout the rooms. It was a terrifying battle between the living and the dead.

It seemed to work, but it actually didn't. The Copelands' ghosts appeared and shot both the priest and the father and locked a crying Linda in another room.

The next morning, the police found the bodies and Linda, but they believed it was a murder-suicide. At the station, Linda was put into the care of a children's home.

Then a week later, a woman told her, 'Linda, I have good news. I found you a new home with a nice mommy and daddy.'

And Linda said, 'I can't wait to meet them.'

https://skobeloff.uk/